Nanny for the Billionaire

A Forced Proximity Off-Limits Romance

Kelly Thomas

BLANK SLATE PUBLICATIONS

Foreward

I'm a nanny for a high-powered billionaire attorney.

But one passionate night changes *everything*...

He hired me to care for his children but I fell for him instead.

Michael, my billionaire boss, is 6'3" of irresistible masculinity.

His vivid green eyes and sexy smile make me forget he's off-limits.

One wild, hot night, we lose control. Now I'm pregnant with his baby.

He marries me out of duty, but I want more than a marriage of convenience.

I'm devoted to him and his family, yet he keeps me at arm's length.

Our chemistry is undeniable, but when I get close, he pulls away.

I'm not interested in just heating up the sheets. I want to set his heart on fire.

No matter how hard I try, he keeps shutting me out.

I should be happy…

I have everything I ever wanted—almost.

Getting Michael to admit he loves me? That's the biggest challenge of all.

Copyright © 2024 by Kelly Thomas

All rights reserved.

No part of this publication may be reproduced, distributed, or transmitted in any form or by any means, including photocopying, recording, or other electronic or mechanical methods, without the prior written permission of the publisher, except as permitted by U.S. copyright law. For permission requests, contact Blank Slate Publications.

The story, all names, characters, and incidents portrayed in this production are fictitious. No identification with actual persons (living or deceased), places, buildings, and products is intended or should be inferred.

Contents

1. One — 1
2. Two — 11
3. Three — 22
4. Four — 31
5. Five — 40
6. Six — 49
7. Seven — 59
8. Eight — 68
9. Nine — 76
10. Ten — 84
11. Eleven — 92
12. Twelve — 103

13.	Thirteen	114
14.	Fourteen	123
15.	Fifteen	132
16.	Sixteen	144
17.	Seventeen	153
18.	Eighteen	163
19.	Nineteen	172
20.	Twenty	183
21.	Twenty-One	193
22.	Twenty-Two	203
23.	Twenty-Three	212
24.	Twenty-Four	221
25.	Twenty-Five	230
26.	Twenty-Six	240
27.	Twenty-Seven	248
28.	Twenty-Eight	258
29.	Twenty-Nine	267
30.	Thirty	275
31.	Thirty-One	285
32.	Thirty-Two	294

33.	Thirty-Three	303
34.	Thirty-Four	312
35.	Thirty-Five	321
36.	Thirty-Six	330
37.	Thirty-Seven	340
38.	Thirty-Eight	352
39.	Thirty-Nine	360
40.	Epilogue	367
	Did you like this Book?	370

One

Michael

Why the hell is it so hard to find a nanny? Discouragement floods through me as I survey the stack of resumes. Each boasts impeccable qualifications and glowing recommendations, yet none spark a flicker of hope. What was I missing? Why don't I like any of them?

I rake my fingers through my hair, the familiar motion offering little comfort.

Damn. None of the nannies I've interviewed seemed like a good fit for my kids.

My disappointment feels overwhelming. I knew finding a nanny would be challenging, but the reality is soul-crushing.

When my late wife, Michelle, died, my world came crashing to a halt. My children were so distraught they clung to me. They needed me. Back then, I didn't want a stranger in the house, and I knew that no one could ever take Michelle's place, so I foolishly thought I could handle my job as a senior partner in a prestigious law firm as well as be there for my children.

That lasted about six months, and then, right in the middle of a high-profile criminal case, Megan, my seven-year-old daughter, decided to skip school. So, I left. I walked out on a case. It was the first time I had ever put my personal life before my profession.

The very next day, I was ordered to the head office by the founding partners. They gave me an ultimatum to hire a nanny or reconsider my position in their firm. I almost walked out. I don't need the money. I could set up my own private practice... but I happen to love what I do and where I do it. The reason I didn't walk out is because—I agreed with them.

They were right, damn it. It wasn't fair to my client. It was a criminal case. He needed me. Fortunately, the judge knew about Michelle. He decided to adjourn the case that day. I was lucky. Damn lucky. That won't happen again. I can't let it happen again.

I wearily examine the paper in my hand.

I'm down to the last interviewee. Her name is Mary Catherine Mitchell. I wince. What a name. It sounds like a good old-fashioned Catholic name. She's probably just like all the others—an uptight middle-aged woman who rarely smiles. So far, every one of the ladies I've interviewed came in wearing a business suit, and some of them didn't even seem interested in hearing about the children.

They just asked about hours, pay, and days off but never about their charges. The only lady who did seem like she might have worked out immediately turned down the job when she read the condition that this was a live-in arrangement. I explained about the attached studio apartment, but she gave me a look that made me feel like a pervert, stuck her offended nose in the air, and left. Good riddance.

I close my eyes. 'Michelle, Love, I miss you so much. You made raising our children look easy. I... I can't seem to do this without you. Please, help me find someone. I just need a nanny who will actually be there for our kids."

I open my eyes, wondering if my desperate words can actually make it to the spirit world. To heaven, as that's where my wife is. She had a heart of gold. She was a great person, a loving wife, and a good soul. I heard once that only the good die young. Now, I believe it. Cancer sucks. My wife deserved a better death.

A sigh escapes my lips. Oh well. Let's get this final interview over with.

I look down at the resume and read it over. When I get to the job history, I give a frown as I see what is written in that field. 'Oldest of six children' and nothing else listed. What the hell? I turn the form over but can't find any other provided jobs or experience.

I look at the references field. Trent Goldman. He's a colleague of mine. In fact, he's the newest junior partner at the law firm.

I think back to when we passed in the hall last week. Trent mentioned something about a cousin of his who is coming into town and might want to interview. I don't remember any other details; I just told him to give my admin his cousin's resume. Hmm. Okay, this must be her... but he called her by another name... what was it? It was an endearment of some sort. I shrug as I don't remember.

ONE

I hear a knock on my home office door.

"Come in," I state in a firm voice.

I rise to my feet as a young woman enters the room, radiating a casual confidence. Unlike the other applicants, she isn't clad in a power suit. Instead, a pair of dark dress pants and a button-down blouse convey a relaxed professionalism. Her long blonde hair cascades down her shoulders, devoid of adornment. As she approaches, she offers a friendly smile and extends out her hand.

"Mr. Garret, it's a pleasure to meet you. I'm Honey Mitchell, Trent Goldman's cousin. Thank you for allowing me to interview for this position."

"Honey, of course. My apologies. I couldn't quite recall your name. Your resume only listed Mary Catherine."

A playful wrinkle forms on her nose. "Southern family tradition. Double first names. Personally, I think it's a bit much."

A genuine laugh escapes my lips. This woman is like a breath of fresh air compared to the formality of the previous interviews.

"Please, have a seat." I gesture toward the chair before my desk as I resume my seat.

As she settles into the chair, I can't help but notice how the golden hues of her name seem to suit her. Her hair shimmers like light honey, and her eyes mirror the deep amber of a cured honeycomb. The young woman exudes a warmth that brightens the entire room. Which is refreshing after the gloom that has clung to my office for weeks,

"Now, I must admit," I begin, "your resume doesn't list much experience. What makes you feel qualified for this position?"

She meets my gaze with an easy smile. "Well, I did list that I'm the oldest of six children. I've been changing diapers and wiping noses since I was a child myself. It's probably the only thing that I'm really good at. And I happen to love children."

She stops with a sheepish smile before she continues, "Sometimes I like them more than adults. When I heard that there was a job posting for a nanny, I thought it would be a good fit."

She glances up at me as she states, "That's what I know how to do. I've had years of experience caring for children. I've just never been paid for it before."

"So, you haven't worked as a nanny before?" I state as a frown furrows my brow. "Any prior work experience at all?"

ONE

"No, sir." She admits, "Not a clock-in, clock-out, paying type of job. I never had time for one. When my mother died, my father had to work. Being the oldest, I took care of the family. Now that everyone is almost grown, they don't really need me anymore."

She takes a breath as she informs me, "So, I decided I wanted to come to Jacksonville. It's a big city, and I was hoping I might be able to find a job. I'm living with my Great-Aunt Skipper right now. Trent's grandma, until I find my feet, as she likes to say."

A flicker of recognition crosses my features. Trent and his wife, Paige, have mentioned his very Southern grandmother.

"I see. Well, thank you for your time, Miss. Mitchell," I begin, attempting to let her down gently. "I appreciate your interest and I have your contact information, so…"

Suddenly, the office door swings open with a bang, and my five-year-old son, Matthew, bolts in, tears streaming down his face and a scraped arm outstretched.

"I fell. I'm bleeding! There's blood!" He wails at the top of his lungs. "It hurts!"

I watch helplessly as Matthew nearly collides with Honey in his frantic dash to get to me.

Before I can react, Honey's calm and soothing voice cuts through the air, "Hey there, little man. Let me see that scrape. How about we blow on it to make the pain go away?"

Matthew skids to a halt, his tear-filled eyes wide with surprise. "Will that work?"

"Absolutely." I watch as Honey reaches into her purse and pulls out a tissue. She gently takes Matthew's scraped elbow. She leans toward him and gently blows on the wound, then smiles at him as she gently wipes away the trace of blood.

"Now, we're not done. You have to tap your nose and pull on your ear if you want the pain to go away," she tells him with a solemn look in her eyes.

I watch as my son seems to forget about his injury. He reaches up, curiously taps his nose, then pulls on his earlobe. He doubtfully tilts his head and says, "It still stings."

"You have to pull harder; give it a good tug," Honey informs him with a nod.

I watch as Matthew pulls on his earlobe harder. His eyes get wide and he looks up at Honey as he says in wonder, "It doesn't hurt as much anymore."

"You just need to spray on some antiseptic and maybe a really large band-aid to keep out the dirt." Honey gives him a wink.

"How large of a band-aid?" Matthew's eyes grow even wider.

"What's the biggest you've got?" Honey asks.

"I don't know." My son turns to me. "Daddy, do we have big band aids?"

"I think so, Matthew. They're in the hall closet in the first aid kit," I tell him.

As I go to get up, my son looks up at Honey. "Will you put it on me and blow on it again?"

"Sure thing. Do you want to show me where the first aid kit is?"

"Uh-huh." He reaches out and takes her hand. He leads her from the chair and out into the hallway. I hear them as they make their way to the hall closet.

I look down at the paper in my hand with a smirk. 'Oldest of six children' really does seem to make her qualified for the job. She sure seems to have my son's vote.

I decide to see what will happen when my more difficult eight-year-old daughter comes home. Losing her mom has really been hard on Megan, and she's not handling the loss well. I sigh as I wish I could reach her and help her with her grief, but she's been mad at the world ever since Michelle died.

I glance at my watch. Megan should be getting home in the next fifteen minutes or so. She stayed late for pre-teen cheerleading practice, and one of the other parents will be dropping her off.

I find Honey and my son sitting at the kitchen table while she positions the biggest band-aid we have in the kit on his arm right below his elbow.

I can still smell the antibacterial spray in the air. My heart beats faster in my chest as I witness this unexpected turn of events. A sliver of hope, fragile yet persistent, begins to grow within me.

Two

Honey

I reach out and gently smooth the band-aid over Matthew's arm. Then I squeeze his hand in a silent promise to make the pain go away. A pang of sympathy shoots through me. He's a doll, all dark curls, and wide, inquisitive green eyes. He's like a miniature version of his father. handsome. Matthew is going to be quite the charmer someday. I just know it.

I inwardly grimace, as I have the distinct feeling that I was being turned down for the job right before Matthew came into the room. I doubt if stopping his son crying is going to change anything. But I've done my duty, and I couldn't just stand by and not help the little tyke out.

I hear the slamming of their front door, and I look up as a disgruntled seven or eight-year-old girl enters the kitchen. She has light brown hair and the biggest blue eyes I've ever seen. But her hair looks... weird. In her hand, she's clutching a bright cheerleading flyer. The girl's blue eyes hold a dullness that mirrors the disheveled state of her hair.

"Hey Megan, how was school?" Michael Garret inquires, his voice laced with concern.

"Fine, Dad," she mumbles, her backpack thudding against the table with a force that speaks volumes about her true feelings. She starts to slink past us, a clear attempt to escape to the privacy of her room. She looks like she wants to cry as she furiously blinks her eyes and frowns down at the floor.

"Megan, could you come over here and meet Honey Mitchell? She's applying for the nanny position," Her father prompts, his voice gentle.

The girl stops short, her lips curling into a slight sneer. "Honey? What kind of a name is that?"

"Well, it's better than Mary Catherine, that's for sure," I say with a friendly lilt in my voice.

She snorts inelegantly. "Really? Your real name is Mary Catherine?"

"Yes, so you can see why Honey seems a whole lot better," I say with a grimace.

"Humph, I guess." She shrugs her shoulders to show she doesn't really care.

Her dad asks, "Megan, how was practice?"

"Fine." She turns abruptly to leave.

There's that fine again, I think to myself.

"So, are you all dressing the same, like the paper you brought home suggested?" He prompts her.

"I don't know, Dad," she says in a voice filled with defeat. "I'm thinking of just quitting the squad."

"What?" His brow crinkles in confusion as he insists, "But you love cheerleading. Why would you quit?"

"We're all supposed to dress the same and wear our hair the same, and I... I... Never mind. I just don't want to do it anymore. That's all," she says in a voice clogged with emotion.

I look at her hair again, and I wonder... "Megan, right? Did the girls decide on a French braid? Because honestly, your hair would look amazing in one."

I glance at her father. "Knowing how to French braid long hair kind of goes with the nanny territory, wouldn't you agree, Mr. Garret? If you want, I can show you my skills by braiding your daughter's hair right now."

I turn back to Megan. "That is, of course, if you'd like me to."

As I see understanding dawn on Mr. Garret's face, he lifts his eyebrows at his daughter, whose face suddenly brightens. He gives me a nod as his daughter sits down on the chair in front of me.

Megan pulls a brush out of her backpack and hands it to me.

"So, what kind of cheers are you doing these days?" I ask curiously as I begin to work on her hair. "Just chants, or are you thinking of tackling some stunts?"

A glimmer of life appears in her eyes. "Mostly chants for now, but Mrs. Jones wants to start teaching us stunts after next week."

I deftly finish the French braid, pick up the rubber band I took out of her hair, and wrap it tightly around the end of the braid. I run my hand down the weaved pieces to make sure they are nice and tight.

With a flourish, I say, "Okay, Megan. Go take a look. See if you like it."

She jumps up and runs into the bathroom.

"Oh my gosh! It's perfect!" Her excited squeal echoes from the bathroom.

A moment later, she bursts back out, a dazzling smile replacing her earlier frown. She spins around, the newly braided hair cascading down her back. "Dad, look! Doesn't it look amazing?"

Mr. Garret's eyes soften as he gazes at his daughter. "Yes, Megan, it looks great."

"Thank you, Honey! This is the best! Can you braid my hair every Wednesday? That's cheerleading practice day," she pleads, her voice brimming with newfound enthusiasm.

My heart swells at the change in her demeanor. This isn't just a job; it's an opportunity to make a difference.

"Well, that depends on your dad," I hedge, trying to maintain a professional demeanor while a flicker of hope has me holding my breath. I glance at Mr. Garret, a silent question hanging in the air.

As if on cue, both Megan and Matthew turn towards their father as well, their eyes wide with hopeful anticipation. Mr. Garret chuckles, the tension from earlier evaporating.

"Well, uh… I still have to run a background check, of course," he begins, rubbing his chin. "But assuming that goes well, I don't see any reason why we shouldn't welcome Miss. Mitchell to the family." He turns to me, a decisive glint in his eyes.

"The job is yours, Miss. Mitchell, if you want it. We can discuss wages, and I can even show you the attached apartment right now if you'd like."

"Yes! Thank you, Mr. Garret!" I say as a delighted smile spreads across my face. My professional facade momentarily forgotten as pure joy bubbles over. "I'd love to see the apartment!"

I look at his children with a big smile. "So, who wants to show me my new home?"

Before I can even blink, I'm caught in a delightful tug-of-war. With all the strength of a five-year-old, Matthew grasps my hand on one side while Megan mirrors him on the other.

Mr. Garret follows behind us at a slower pace.

As I step inside the studio, I'm pleasantly surprised. It's small but feels surprisingly spacious. The kitchenette, though com-

TWO

pact, has everything I need. The bed looks cozy and inviting, and there's a small sitting area by the window. It's a perfect little space to call my own, and I can't wait to make it feel like home.

After the children show me around, Michael Garret asks, "Well, what do you think of the place?"

"It's perfect," I tell him honestly. "I like that I'll have my own entrance and yet will still be close if the children need me."

As we exit the studio apartment, Mr. Garret reminds the children to do their homework before dinner.

Once they wave goodbye and leave, I follow Mr. Garret back to his home office.

"Let's go over your schedule and what will be expected of you," he says with a smile.

I take the list and read it over. "Laundry, cooking, light house cleaning, and grocery shopping," I read aloud, then glance up at him. "Yes, that's what I was expecting."

"Now for your salary," he states my weekly salary, and I try hard to hide my reaction. The amount he quoted is a lot more than I expected. I try not to let my excitement show. But I'm positively thrilled with the salary and the benefits. It will seem like even more without having to pay for an apartment.

"Are you ready to sign the contract?" He asks with a raise of his eyebrow.

"Yes, but Mr. Garret..." I hesitate, and then, with a deep breath, I ask gently, "When did your wife pass, and how is it affecting the children... and you?"

I watch him closely as he gives a heavy sigh and glances up at the ceiling. "I lost my wife a little over six months ago to cancer." His voice falters for a moment, then he continues with a voice laced with sorrow, "Michelle wasn't supposed to get sick or die. We were supposed to grow old together, retire, and travel around the country. We used to laugh about it. That's what we had planned... to grow old together."

He stops to clear his throat, looking a little lost, before he continues in a low voice, "We met right after I graduated from law school. I was eager to prove myself as an attorney." He twists his lips in a semblance of a smile as he admits, "I was so full of myself when I met her. Michelle quickly let me know that she didn't like lawyers. Any lawyers."

He pauses and gets a soft smile on his face before he continues, "I made it my mission to change her mind. And I did. First, I talked her into dating me, and then we got engaged, married, and had children. We were living the dream... Then she was diagnosed with cancer."

Michael Garret stops as if he's already said too much. I give him an encouraging smile, and he continues, "I'm hoping that hiring you as the kid's nanny will restore our family unit. Megan is not handling the loss of her mother well. She's angry at the world... and Matthew... well, he just wants to be loved."

He glances up at me with a sheepish smile. "They're great kids. They just miss their mother, and they're grieving. Without Michelle, our family dynamic is broken. Maybe you can help mend the tear. Only time will tell."

I give him a sincere look. "You know, Mr. Garret, they say the pain of losing a loved one never truly goes away. Instead, it just fades a little every day. I hope I can help speed up the fading."

He nods his head thoughtfully at my words without saying anything in response. However, some of the tightness around his eyes has lessened.

Mr. Garret clears his throat and then, returning to business, silently pulls open a drawer, takes out some paperwork, and hands it to me.

I briefly skim over it. It appears to be a boilerplate contract. When he hands me a pen, I sign my name.

He gives me a nod, as he states, "I should get the results from the background check sometime tomorrow via email."

I grin as I know my background check isn't a concern. I nod, stand and he shakes my hand.

He offers with a slight smile, "You can move in over the weekend if you'd like. Then officially start next Monday morning."

"Thank you," I say, knowing my eyes are gleaming with satisfaction.

As I leave to get into my bright yellow Volkswagen Beetle, he reminds me, "I'll get you added to my car insurance. You'll have the use of an older SUV for picking up the children."

I can only nod. This just keeps getting better and better. Once he's turned to go back into the house, I reach out and give my small car a loving pat.

Now, my last worry is gone. I had some concerns about my Volkswagen being big enough for the children and their gear. I drove a minivan back home, but when I decided to move away, I bought the little VW Beetle just for me. At the time, I thought my days of taking care of children were over.

TWO

I give a brilliant smile. I have no complaints, as I happen to adore children. I think it's ironic that I came all this way to claim my independence just to do what I was doing back home. I shrug. It's a job and a good-paying one at that!

Michael Garret seems like a very nice man... There is just something about him... his vivid green eyes, dark hair, and chiseled jaw. I don't know his age, but he has a bit of gray around his temples—Just enough to make him look distinguished. He's very attractive... but he's obviously grieving. The entire family seems... broken by their loss.

The intense yearning I feel from deep inside me takes me by surprise. A steely determination comes over me. I want to help this family. I want to help him. I want to help chase the sadness and despair from their eyes and make them whole again.

I feel my smile as it spreads across my face. I head to my Aunt Skipper's house. I can't wait to let my aunt and cousin know I was hired.

Three

Michael

A satisfied sigh escapes my lips as I survey the living room. Honey only moved in today, yet the atmosphere already feels lighter. Playful echoes of laughter replace the heavy silence that had settled after Michelle's passing.

One of the first things I say to her this afternoon is, "I think we should call each other by our first names. My family thrives on informality."

She nods her head. "Okay, Michael."

"Honey, you didn't bring much with you," I remark, noticing the sparse amount of luggage and boxes behind her scattered over the floor.

She shrugs, a simple joy radiating from her smile. "Just the essentials."

I see clothes, books, maybe a few too many pairs of shoes. "That's not that much," I say simply.

She shrugs, "It's a good thing not having too many material things."

I chuckle, a genuine sound that surprises even me. "Honey, you're unlike any nanny I ever imagined hiring, and yet, you seem to be exactly what this family needs." She follows me into the bright kitchen.

"Thank you, Mr. Garret—Sorry, Michael." She then says softly, "I hope my being here can help them adjust to being without their mother."

The patter of smaller feet announces the return of the children. I glance around, grateful for the interruption. The conversation has drifted towards a territory that's still raw and painful.

"Just grabbing some lemonade," Matthew announces, his voice buzzing with the energy of a young boy on the move.

With their departure, I turn toward Honey and sigh, the weight of grief still clinging to me. "I had no clue what was bothering Megan," I admit, the words tumbling out before I can stop them. "But you figured it out and fixed it with a simple braid. Who knew that knowing how to style hair was a skill I would need?"

A bittersweet smile plays on Honey's lips. "Michael, being a good father doesn't require braiding expertise. You have the qualities that truly matter - love, patience, and a fierce desire to see your children happy."

My heart aches with a familiar pang. "They miss their mother," I rasp, the words raw with emotion. "The cancer poisoned everything it touched. By the end, I think Michelle was ready to go. She was so tired and weak." I glance over at Honey. "She only held on for us, the kids and me. Michelle faced it all with such courage, never once complaining, always putting on a brave face."

A flicker of empathy softens Honey's gaze. "Losing her must have been devastating," she says softly, her voice laced with a genuine understanding.

THREE

For the first time, talking about Michelle doesn't feel like an exercise in self-torture. Perhaps it's the empathy in Honey's eyes, a silent acknowledgment of the pain that's become my constant companion.

"Yes, it was," I confess, the words tumbling out in a wave of pent-up emotion. "Only once did I see her broken. Broken so completely that I couldn't console her. Michelle had found the little purse she carried at our wedding. She said her mother had given it to her as something old."

Honey's brow furrows in understanding. "Oh, yes. Something old, something new, something borrowed, something blue," she murmurs, a knowing smile gracing her lips.

"Yes," I croak, the memory vivid even after all this time. "Michelle told me about a family tradition where the mother gives the daughter the heirloom purse the night before the wedding. She sobbed, heartbroken that she wouldn't be there when Megan walked down the aisle. It ripped her apart."

I look over at Honey, seeking some type of solace. "Watching her become that emotional broke my heart, too. Cancer is a terrible disease that viciously destroys. I promised her that Megan would be given the purse, but I knew it wasn't the same. Michelle wanted so desperately to live so she could be there for our daughter's special moment."

Honey offers a sad smile, a silent acknowledgment of the limitations of words in the face of such profound loss.

"Michael, that's a heart-wrenching story," she says with sincerity, "I'm glad you were able to promise Michelle that you'd give the purse to Megan before she walks down the aisle. Did that comfort her?" She asks softly.

"A little. I also gave her some paper and a pen and asked her to write down what she would want to say to Megan on that day. I have it hidden with her pearl-encrusted purse in a box in the closet. When that day comes, Megan will have something from her mother."

Honey offers a sad smile, her eyes welling up slightly. She nods knowingly, a silent acknowledgment that sometimes words simply aren't enough.

As I turn to leave, my mind drifts back to those final days with Michelle. The cancer, a monstrous entity, had devoured everything in its path. It ravaged Michelle and nearly took me with it. A part of me craved the oblivion it offered, the chance to join Michelle.

But the children needed a parent. With a gentle hand, Michelle reminded me of that responsibility, a final act of love before the darkness claimed her. So, I lived—each day a struggle to get out of bed without her, the ache in my heart a constant companion.

The grief still haunts me. Simply put, I miss my wife.

"Michelle," I whisper, my voice thick with emotion, "I hope this nanny works out. But my love, no one can ever take your place."

It's Monday, the official first day for Honey to start as the kids' nanny. When I walk downstairs, I find her already in the kitchen. She's looking through all the kitchen cabinets. She's dressed in blue jeans and a simple top. Her honey-colored hair is down around her shoulders. I glance down and notice she's barefoot. My mind conjures up a picture of Michelle, she liked to run around without shoes in the house. Will everything Honey does remind me of what I've lost?

I roughly clear my throat. "Did you find what you're looking for?"

"Oh, good morning, Mr. Garret. I was just trying to figure out where everything is."

"Honey, you're supposed to be calling me Michael. We're pretty informal around here."

"I forgot, sorry... Michael. Do you want cereal or a cooked breakfast?" She glances at me over her shoulder.

"On the weekdays, I normally just have a cup of coffee. I grab a bagel or toast at work. On the weekends, though, we normally have a big hot breakfast. I like just about anything." I give her a grin. "The kids aren't that picky regarding breakfast foods. But I do think blueberry pancakes are a favorite."

She grins back. "I'll keep that in mind. And the children, do they typically have cold cereal every morning?"

"Yes. Count Chocula is Matthew's current favorite cereal. I think Megan still prefers Fruit Loops, but it can change on a dime."

"Understood." She grins as amusement fills her eyes.

I watch as Honey sets everything on the table. I leave her to it while I get my briefcase. She fills up my travel mug with fresh hot coffee, and I nod my thanks.

"Okay, I'm going to leave you with the kids. Thanks for dropping them off. They know the drill and can tell you where to park and everything." I assure her, "I've already filled out all the forms, so the school will know you'll pick them up and drop them off daily. Call me if you need me."

"I think we'll be fine. Thank you, Mr....um. Michael." She gives me a reassuring smile.

I turn at the door to say, "Oh, I almost forgot. Here's a credit card. Use this for any expenses. Groceries, school clothes, cleaning stuff... let me know if you have any questions. Do keep the receipts. You can put them in this drawer, and I'll check them as I need them."

Honey nods. She seems very competent, and her driving record is impeccable. I don't know why I'm still hanging around. Maybe because things are just now starting to feel normal again.

I hear Matthew on the stairs. He bounds down them and comes barreling into the kitchen.

"I'm starving," he announces to the room at large and then sits down and begins to pour milk over his cereal.

Megan comes into the kitchen next. She has her hair pulled back into a high ponytail. She sits down and starts fixing herself a bowl of Fruit Loops. She rolls her eyes at my son's impression of Count Chocula. I hear them begin to banter back and forth.

I shake my head. One minute, Megan's acting like a child, and the next, she's acting like a thirty-year-old. I smile. This is what I was waiting around for. Our typical family mornings like they used to be when Michelle was still alive.

I go over and give each of my children a hug, and then I leave. As I get in my car, I realize that for the first time in a long time, I truly feel like my kids are going to be okay.

Hiring Honey just feels right.

Four

Honey

It's been two weeks since I started. I can't believe how quickly the time has flown. I glance around the kitchen making sure I have everything I need ready to go.

My phone chimes, and as I look down, I see my Great-Aunt Skipper is calling.

"Honey, how is everything going with you and the Garret family?"

"Hey Aunt Skipper. Everything is going fine. We've settled into a routine," I reply. "I get up before the children, they feed themselves, and then I drop them off at school." I tuck my cell phone between my chin and shoulder so I can finish wiping down the counter.

I continue, "After that, I have some free time just to relax, but I typically come home and do my cleaning and household chores or pick up groceries."

My aunt asks, "So, do you like the job? I already know you're great with children."

"Yes, I'm really enjoying being their nanny. Almost every afternoon, I pick up Matthew and Megan from their school," I tell her my schedule. "On days like Wednesday, when Megan has pre-teen cheerleading practice, some of the children's parents and I have a rotating schedule where we take turns driving them home after practice. So, I normally don't have to worry about picking up Megan on those days unless it's my turn to carpool for the entire cheerleading squad."

"Well, that doesn't sound too bad." I hear a chuckle in her voice.

"No, it isn't. Last week, I went on a field trip as a chaperon for Matthew's classroom. It was fun. The kids are great, too. Michael seems to be a very good father, and Michelle must have been a wonderful mother as her children are well-behaved. The kids, my charges, are fun to be around."

FOUR

"You make them sound like little saints," she says with a hint of dryness.

I laugh in response. "Oh no, believe me, they are not saints! They can be rascals! It's only to be expected as kids learn how to be responsible for themselves. So, sometimes they have to test their wings, which can try my patience, but then they go right back to being... well, kids. Happy-go-lucky kids. Which is how things should be," I say, my voice filled with satisfaction.

My Aunt Skipper's voice softens as she states, "I'm sure they miss their mother. What about their father, is he nice?"

"Yes, Michael's very nice, and kind. He's been wonderful! And so understanding, too!"

My aunt mutters, "You don't say—"

"Oh, Aunt Skipper, I just noticed the time. I have to run some cupcakes to Matthew's class."

"Alright, Honey. I'll talk to you later."

After our goodbyes, I grab the container of cupcakes and drive to Matthew's school. When I enter his classroom with the baked goods, his teacher, Mrs. Kelsey, gratefully takes the treats out of my hands.

"Thanks! The munchkins are getting restless," she comments with an eye roll.

I give her a friendly grin as I explain. "They're cupcakes for Matthew Garret."

His teacher gives me an appraising glance. "Oh, so you must be the new nanny. How do you like the job?"

"Yes, I'm the new nanny; I'm Honey Mitchell. The job? I love it. They are great kids."

"I knew their mother. Michelle was a really nice person. I know the entire family has been grieving her loss." Mrs. Kelsey gives me an earnest look as she continues, "Honey, I've noticed a difference in the last two weeks. Matthew seems... more like his old self."

She gives me a friendly smile. "I know a nanny can't take the place of his mother. I mean, no one can. But I think just having you around, having someone to be there for him... I can tell it's helping him cope. He seemed so lost before."

I feel a wave of happiness wash over me at her words. "Thanks. I'm glad I'm making a difference. It's hard, but kids are so resilient. They're amazing, aren't they?"

FOUR

His teacher's smile widens. "Wow, you do like children. I can tell." She offers, "If you ever give up on being a nanny, we could surely use someone with your attitude around here."

I spend the rest of the day helping pass out cupcakes and handing out art supplies. It's a good afternoon, filled with the carefree laughter of the children and the smell of paste and crayons.

Once school is out, Matthew and I wait in the car for Megan to join us.

The car door opens, and Megan climbs in with her backpack.

"I've got a roast in the crockpot, so there's no urgency to get home. Do you guys want Dairy Queen?" I ask, turning to the children in the backseat.

"Sure!" they both respond enthusiastically.

I smile as they settle into their seats. I drive us to the local Dairy Queen. We walk in and place our order. Matthew gets a chocolate malt, and Megan and I order a dipped cone. As we slide into a booth, I savor the creamy sweetness of my ice cream.

"So, how was school, Megan?" I ask, turning to her.

Her eyes gleam with excitement. "It was good. Art is my favorite class. We made things out of clay this week."

"That sounds like fun. Will you be able to bring home your artwork? I'm sure your dad would love to see what you made." I smile at her, adding, "And I would, too."

"Yeah, he always tells me how good I am at art, but then he doesn't know what it is. Last year, I made him a little horse. He thought it was a dog. Mom..." Megan stops talking, her voice trailing off.

"Go on, Megan, what about your mom?" I say softly, reaching out to squeeze her hand.

"Well, Mom could always tell what they were. She knew it was a horse and not a dog." Megan looks down at her hands. "I miss her. Dad tries, he tries really hard, but he doesn't know some things... like how to fix my hair, and you know, other stuff... because he's a dad. I miss my mom," she admits as she blinks the wetness from her lashes.

I give them both a direct look. "It's okay, you know, to miss her," I assure them softly. "I lost my mom when I was your age. I remember it was really hard."

"You did?" Meghan looks up at me with wide eyes.

"Yeah, I did. So, while it's different for everyone, I can relate to how you feel."

"I miss Mommy too," Matthew says in a sad little voice and wipes his nose on his sleeve. I give him a soft smile as I hand him a napkin.

Then, I turn to them with an earnest tone in my voice. "It's okay, you know, to miss her," I assure them, my voice reassuring, "I used to write my mom letters. I felt it was a way that I could continue talking to her. She couldn't talk back, of course. But it was a way for me to continue to share my experiences with her. Anyway, that helped me as I was growing up."

When Matthew gives a small frown, I continue in a soft voice, "It's also okay to be happy and not miss her." When I glance at them, I see that they're both listening intently with solemn faces. "Sometimes, I would feel guilty because I would forget to miss my mother. I had to allow myself to be content without thinking about her."

I lean back against the hard plastic bench. "I think that's what all mothers want for their children: for them to live their lives every day and just be happy." I glance at them both, wanting my words to make a difference. "I think that's what your mom would also want for you."

They both look thoughtful as they mull over my words. It's mostly silent as we finish our treats. Gone is the carefree laughter when I picked them up from school. Instead, I can see their pain. Their loss is written plainly on their faces.

I so want to help them with their grief. Baby steps, I remind myself. What I really want to do—is scoop them both into a loving hug and protect them from all of life's ups and downs.

My lips twist into a grimace. For now, I can at least give them a safe haven to come home to.

"Okay, everybody in the car. Let's get this show on the road," I announce instead.

Matthew scrunches up his face and says, "Honey, you sure talk funny sometimes."

"Yeah, I know." I grin down at him. "I'm a Southern gal, Matthew. We have a lot of funny sayings in the South."

When we approach the car, I finally give in to my emotions. With a warm embrace, I gather the children into my arms, holding them close.

As Matthew hugs me back, he asks in a small voice, "What's that for, Honey?"

"Not a thing, Matthew. It's just because I can," I say in an exaggerated Southern draw. "Yep. Just because I can."

He smiles up at me while Megan rolls her eyes, but I notice she doesn't try to pull away.

"Come on, let's all go home."

Five

TWO YEARS LATER

Honey

I pick up the kids, and we head to Dairy Queen. It's our Thursday after-school ritual.

"Matt, you want a chocolate malt or..." I ask him.

"Yeah. A chocolate malt, please," he mumbles as he bounds across the restaurant to find us a booth. Megan and I approach the counter to order.

Once we have our treat, we walk to the booth and slide in. I hand Matthew his malt, and Megan and I both lick our dipped cones.

I look at Matthew. "So, how was school?"

"I don't like Social Studies. It sucks!" He says with a scowl.

"Ha. Social Studies is a breeze compared to beginning algebra. Algebra sucks more," Megan tells him.

I let the kids banter back and forth about their schoolwork and give a contented smile as I lean back in my seat and continue to eat my ice cream cone.

Thursdays are always the same. A roast in the crockpot, a quick stop at Dairy Queen, and then to the house so the kids can finish their homework. I ensure we have these carefree moments to share every week.

I look over at Matthew and notice he needs his hair trimmed. It's getting a little too long and starting to hang over his eyes.

Megan's hair is in a French braid, even though she didn't have practice today. I smile as she can really rock a braid. Her hair is very long now, but she doesn't want to cut it. I can see why. She has beautiful, thick, glossy brown hair.

Matthew's growing like a weed. He's tall, like his dad—Michael's six foot three. I wonder if Michelle was tall. It's hard to tell from the family portraits. I'll have to make a mental note to take Matt clothes shopping soon before he outgrows everything he's got. I might as well look for shoes, too. Matthew is like a carbon copy of his handsome father; he has the same thick dark hair and vivid green eyes. They share some of the same mannerisms as well.

I glance at the time and say, "Come on, let's get this show on the road."

We all pile into the car, and I drive us home. It's been a hectic week as I had to carpool for the cheerleading squad twice. Megan loves being on the squad, so I don't complain. Between her cheerleading and Matthew starting to run track, I have to juggle my time to make all their practices.

When we arrive home, the kids run upstairs to finish their homework. I get the table set for supper and glance at the clock. Michael should be home in about half an hour. He's always hungry when he gets home, so I try to serve supper quickly.

As I lift the lid on the roast, a mouthwatering aroma escapes, filling the kitchen. Replacing the lid, I toss together a fresh salad, sprinkling it generously with almonds. Michael and the kids adore almonds. I then grab their favorite salad dressings, a tangy vinaigrette for the guys and me, and a creamy ranch for Megan.

I also grilled asparagus as a side, as it's Michael's favorite. He likes my roast with extra gravy for his mashed potatoes. I get everything ready to be served. I hear the front door open. It's Michael. I glance up eagerly as he comes through the door.

He gives me an easy smile as he sets down his briefcase. "Hi Honey, how's everything going? Are the kids doing okay?"

My eyes take in his dark hair and the intense green of his eyes. As I answer in a slightly breathy voice, "Yes, Matthew doesn't like Social Studies, and Megan hates Algebra, but otherwise, everything is right with the world."

Michael smiles. "Good." He sniffs the air appreciatively. "That pot roast sure smells good."

I turn to him with a brilliant smile as my eyes drift over his handsome features. "How are things going at the law firm?"

Michael hesitates and then shrugs, "Same old. Same old." He then changes the subject. "When will dinner be ready? I'm hungry."

I turn around with a platter of roast beef piled high. "It's ready now. I just need to get the food on the table." He helps me carry the remaining dishes to the dining room.

"Okay, kids. Time to eat," I yell softly up the stairwell. Soon, I hear their footsteps clamoring down the stairs.

We all gather around the table and sit down to eat. This is my second favorite time of the day. Dinner with the entire family. Michael dishes up the food and turns to the children. "So, what's wrong with Social Studies and Algebra?"

The children each give an audible groan. Matthew, with his usual enthusiasm, describes his struggles with the class. Megan, ever the practical one, counters with her disdain for math, algebra in particular. Meanwhile, their father listens attentively, occasionally interjecting with a thoughtful comment or a humorous anecdote. The warmth of the dining room, combined with the delicious food and the lively conversation, creates our typical perfect family dinner.

As we each finish the meal, I stand and get the hot apple pie I made as a surprise for Michael. It's his favorite. "I made pie for dessert. I hope you still have room." I place it on the table.

Michael gives me a wide smile. "Apple pie! Great. Thank you, Honey. I'm sure it tastes as good as it looks."

I give him a warm smile at the compliment.

FIVE

All of us find room for the sweet dessert. After everyone leaves the table, I gather the dishes and place them in the dishwasher. I hum softly to myself as I clean up the kitchen.

Michael and the kids are in the family room. I pop my head in and say, "Good night, everyone. I'll be in my apartment if you need me for anything."

Michael glances up in surprise. "Honey, it's early. You don't want to watch TV with us?"

I shake my head. "Not tonight. I'm saying goodnight early because I want to send some emails to my family back home."

Michael nods his eyes on the television screen. "Okay, good night, Honey."

I shut my door, sit down at my laptop, and type out a few emails to my family. They like hearing about Michael and the children; otherwise, I don't have that much to tell them. I make sure to send a separate email to my grandfather. He's the head of our family, and his health isn't what it used to be. He has a caregiver who has watched over my grandfather for as long as I can remember. Wherever my grandfather is, Lock is too. He's like a silent sentinel watching over him.

A feeling of nostalgia washes over me as I think about my family. I love them, and occasionally I get homesick. I haven't visited them in over a year. I wonder how all of my younger siblings are doing. Who is doing what, and all the little things that make up a family. The girls do a better job of keeping me updated than the boys. I grin as I picture my family members in my mind. I really should make an effort to visit them all soon. But for now, emails and texts are the easiest ways to stay in touch.

As I describe the Garret family, I suddenly frown. Now that I think about it. Michael seemed quiet. It's like he had something on his mind tonight. A frown crosses my face as I wonder how things are going at the law firm. He didn't bring it up over dinner, which is unusual for him. The other night, he mentioned that a colleague had flown in to talk to him about taking over a case. It sounded last minute. He typically enjoys sharing some of the funnier things that happen at the law firm where he works with the family.

I smile as I think of my favorite time of day. It's when the kids are in bed and Michael and I are alone and sit at the table and softly discuss the day. We talk about the children and anything else that comes up. It's always pleasant to spend time with him. I like to listen to his deep voice as we discuss different topics.

Tomorrow is my night off. I picked that day because the kids will be out of the house. Megan is off to a birthday slumber

FIVE

party, and Matthew will be at a friend's sleepover. I've got everything sorted - permission slips signed, pickups arranged.

I've also got a date with Colton, my boyfriend of a few months. He's a good-looking blonde. He's very stylish and prides himself on being a foodie. He plans on taking me to a fancy five-star restaurant. I had better pick out something nice to wear if he's going to all that trouble. I guess I'll dress for him tomorrow night. He always likes it when I make an effort.

I bit my lip as I search through my closet, looking for the perfect outfit. I finally come to a sand-colored dress that is a very simple design. It doesn't look like much until you put it on, then it shimmers as I move and is sexy as hell. It fits me like a glove and hugs my curves in an almost indecent way.

I have matching shoes somewhere. I get them out of the closet and then look for the earrings I always wear with this ensemble. The earrings are long and dangly, they look like the inside of a seashell. I don't get the opportunity to wear this outfit very often as it's a little too suggestive.

I shrug. It may put Colton in a better mood. He loves it when I wear sexy clothes. I shake my head as I remember that he doesn't mind me wearing jeans as long as I have on high heels. I'd prefer to wear sneakers or flip-flops with my jeans, but Colton likes the look of me in heels.

I suddenly frown as I realize I've slowly been changing how I dress to please him.

Lately, Colton's been acting increasingly possessive, which bothers me. He's started complaining that I rarely shed my nanny persona and responsibilities. I don't appreciate his controlling behavior. He's also been demanding more of my time and seems resentful of the hours I spend with the Garrets. He gets impatient whenever I mention my charges or anything related to the family. It's making me feel very uncomfortable.

Six

Michael

It's the next day, a Friday, and it's almost five o'clock, the end of my work day. I see a co-worker, Jeff, walking toward me.

"Hey, Michael. Colleen was asking about you again today. When are you planning on getting back in the dating pool, man?"

My eyes widen in surprise at the question. "I haven't really thought about it, Jeff. Michelle has only been gone a couple of years."

He shrugs with his hands. "That's a long time, Michael. Colleen is a very nice lady, and she's hot as hell, if you know what I mean." He jiggles his eyebrows with a slight leer. "You ought to at least consider taking her out."

"Colleen does seem to be interested," I say carefully. Then I frown at him as I explain, "I just don't know if I'm ready to start dating yet. Besides, I don't know how my kids would react if I started seeing someone."

Jeff puts his hand on my shoulder. "Michael, Colleen asked me to invite you out for a drink. Cynthia and I will be there too, so think of it more like a get-together after work. We're going to invite a few other couples as well."

I feel a pang of irritation at his persistence. "When?" I ask flatly.

"Tonight. She wanted us all to get together around seven o'clock at the Hilton. They have a nice bar at the hotel where she's staying while she's in town. It would be a good opportunity for you guys to possibly hook up." As I continue to frown, Jeff shrugs. "At the very least, she might be able to send more business our way. It's always nice to network and get your name out there, Michael."

I finally give a reluctant nod. "Jeff, I can't promise I'll be there, but I'll try and make it."

He slaps me on the back with a smirk. "Great. Hope to see you there," he says as I turn toward my office.

SIX

It's been a long day, and I'd like nothing better than to relax at home. But when I get back to my office, I decide to look over the file of the case I've been asked to represent, though I haven't been given all of the details yet. They only provided this one file, which is frustrating. I've been promised more information in the near future. The kids are both staying with friends tonight, and Honey has the night off.

She's probably going out tonight with that young guy she's been seeing. I wonder if it's getting serious between them. Surely not, as the guy seems to be a pompous ass if you ask me. He doesn't seem nice enough for her.

I frown as Honey's been dating him for several months, now. I've seen him pick her up in some fancy, low-slung sports car. Every time I see him in that damn car, I think he must be overcompensating for a physical shortcoming—I give a grim smile as I ruefully shake my head. I really think she could do better, but then I realize that I'm judging the guy solely by the car he drives and how he looks, as I've never actually met him in person.

I go back to the file as I have no desire to go home to an empty house tonight. By the time I look up again, I see that it's a quarter after six.

I grimace as I remember that I told Jeff I'd try to stop by the Hilton bar. Maybe he's right. Maybe I just need to take the plunge and ask Colleen out. Why am I so hesitant to get back into the dating pool?

The decision made, I push away from my desk. I have nothing else to do, so why not drink with some colleagues and talk with an attractive woman?

The Hilton bar is a sleek, sophisticated space bathed in soft, golden light. A long, polished mahogany bar dominates the room, its surface gleaming under the low-hanging lights. Comfortable leather chairs are arranged around high-top tables, providing a rich atmosphere for patrons to relax and socialize. The air is filled with the gentle hum of conversation and the clinking of glasses.

The bar is already starting to fill up as I enter. I scan the room, spotting Jeff and his girlfriend, Cynthia. Then, my gaze falls on Colleen. She's dressed in a sharp blue power suit that accentuates her brown hair and eyes. Her overly eager gaze, however, sends a chill down my spine. While I don't mind a woman taking the initiative, I don't appreciate feeling pushed or pressured.

As I approach, Collen's eyes gleam her welcome. "Michael. I'm glad you could make it."

SIX

"Hi, Colleen, Jeff, Cynthia." I nod to each of them. Then I glance around. "Is anyone else from the firm here tonight?"

Collen gestures to the empty seat beside hers. "Not yet, Michael. Why don't you have a seat?"

I sit and order a scotch, then offer to buy Colleen a drink. Once we receive our order, Colleen gives me a sultry smile as she picks up her glass and takes a sip.

I'm not quite sure what game Colleen's playing, but I'm willing to find out. I sit there quietly, nursing my scotch as I listen to the other three's conversation. I give the occasional nod, but otherwise, I don't feel any desire to join in.

I feel Colleen press her leg against mine and see her glance at me under her lashes. I raise a dark brow at her inquiringly. She just smiles and presses her leg even harder against mine.

I may have been out of the dating game for a while, but I know when a woman wants me. And Colleen makes it very obvious she finds me attractive. I just don't think that's all she desires.

I see Jeff give me a look, and then he pulls Cynthia over to the bar. He turns around and gives me a thumbs-up. I give an inward sigh. He thinks he's my wingman.

I glance over at Colleen. She leans in closer to me and says, "Alone at last."

I give her an assessing look. She's too calculating in a predatory way. She may be attracted to me, but she wants something more.

I decide to put my cards on the table and just ask her, "So, Colleen, what game are you playing here? What is it you want from me?"

"Why, Michael, I thought it was pretty obvious what I... want. You're a very tempting man. I thought I was making it clear. I certainly wouldn't mind spending the night with you. I have a room here at the hotel while I'm in town if you're interested," she says slyly, evading my true question.

"And is that all you want, Colleen?" I ask her gruffly. "I can tell a player when I see one. Maybe you want something behind the scenes. So, why don't you just tell me and make this easier for both of us?"

She gives me a childish pout. "Where's the fun in that, Michael?"

I feel her lean in and boldly brush against me. My body responds in spite of my negative feelings toward the woman. But damn, it's been a long time since I've had a woman. I turn away.

SIX

She doesn't need to know that my body's responding to her nearness.

I spend the next hour ignoring her subtle and not-so-subtle advances. Thankfully Jeff and Cynthia decide to again join us at the table, and everyone is talking shop.

I glance at my watch. I'm beyond ready to leave. Colleen gives me another assessing look and then leans in one more time in a final attempt to get me up to her room.

She bends forward and gives me a kiss on the side of my cheek as she whispers, "You wouldn't regret it, Micheal. I'd make sure of that."

"I don't doubt it for a minute," I respond drily.

Just then, my phone rings. When I answer it, I hear Lisa Johnson, a parent, she's frantic.

"Michael. I'm so sorry! It's Matthew; he fell out of our tree house. I think he may have broken his arm. We're on the way to the downtown Baptist hospital right now."

"I'll meet you there shortly." I try to calm my racing heart as worry for Matthew courses through me. "Thanks for informing me, Lisa. Take care of my son."

I disconnect the line. "I have to go. My son's been injured. They're taking him to the hospital now."

Jeff gives me a look of concern. "Oh no, man, that's tough. Of course, you have to go. Hope he's going to be okay."

I hear their well wishes as I hurriedly exit the bar. I'm halfway across the lobby when I see Honey. At least, I think that's Honey... She's dressed in a figure-hugging slinky dress that leaves very little to the imagination. I feel my body respond with a vengeance.

Right now, she looks distraught. "Honey?" I stammer as I approach her.

She abruptly turns toward me, and I see her shoulders slump in relief. "Oh, Michael. Matthew's hurt; they're taking him to Baptist hospital."

I nod. "I know. I just got the call; I'm on the way there now."

She suddenly studies my face and then glances behind me, noticing where I came from. She gives me a frown and a look filled with disapproval.

A confused frown furrows my brow. "Honey, were you on a date tonight?"

"Yes, I was, but we need to get to Matthew." Then, with an urgent plea in her voice, "He's hurt. He needs us."

"Come on, I'll drive us there," I state firmly.

As we turn to leave, her date stalks out of the Hilton's restaurant. He moves toward Honey, a scowl on his face. "I meant what I said, Mary Catherine. It's over between us if you leave," he offers the ultimatum in a grim voice. "I can't have my fiancée running off to be with an older man and his family whenever anything happens. Not when she should be with me."

Honey turns around and looks up at him with an angry glare. "I guess you didn't hear my response to your proposal. So, I'll say it again: No, thank you, Colton." She continues in an icy voice, "I prefer to live my life my way. I am no man's arm candy, and Matthew needs me. I'm leaving now."

I give the younger guy a hard look. Then I turn to her. "Come on, Honey. Let's go."

"I knew you had something going on with your boss." I hear the sneer and insult in his voice. "Nobody is that devoted to their job."

I turn back around and say in a deadly quiet voice, "Colton? I don't have time to put you in your place. But I won't allow you to insult Honey like that. The next time we meet, you will apologize to her, or you'll answer to me. Got it?"

I don't wait for his response. Instead, I take Honey's arm, and we exit the lobby.

We have to get to the hospital.

Seven

Honey

I look up at Michael and ask, "Have you been drinking? Do I need to drive?"

I see him grimace. "I've only had one drink. A scotch, I'm fine to drive us."

He escorts me to his car and opens the door for me, and I slide into the seat. The high split in my dress opens and shows off a good amount of my bare thigh. I feel Michael's eyes on my exposed skin.

He hurries around the car, gets in, and guns the engine. Then we're on our way to the hospital.

When we get there, we go straight to Emergency. Lisa and her husband meet us in the waiting room.

Lisa looks up in relief. "We didn't have any paperwork with us, so they didn't want to treat him until you got here."

Michael says, "I'm here now."

He approaches the desk and gives them his information. I see him pull out his insurance card, and then he asks if he can see his son.

I hear the nurse assure him. "Of course, Mr. Garret."

"Honey, I'll go check on Matthew. You'll be here?" I nod in response to his question.

The hospital staff calls an orderly who escorts Michael back to his son. I turn toward Lisa and her husband.

"So, you're the nanny?" I give a sharp look at Lisa's husband at his knowing tone.

Lisa elbows her husband and looks at me apologetically. "I think John misinterpreted your name. Honey, this is my husband, John."

I ignore her husband as I ask, "How is Matthew? Is he in a lot of pain?"

SEVEN

"I think so, but he's been a trooper. My oldest son saw Matthew fall out of our tree house. We brought him here as soon as we could. We're so sorry this happened."

I give her a reassuring smile. "It's no one's fault. Kids will be kids."

Lisa looks down at my outfit. "I'm sorry we interrupted your night. Were you on a date?"

"Yes," I say absently, and then I see her husband, John, give a snide grin to his wife. So, I clarify my answer, "With Colton Johns, my boyfriend. At least, he was... my boyfriend." I shake my head. "I don't know anymore, as he didn't want me to leave, but I had to get to Matthew. Anyway, Michael happened to be in the bar and saw me leaving the restaurant. So, I rode here with him."

Lisa and John nod, but I don't care what they think about my situation. I only care about Matthew right now. I love him and his sister deeply.

I glance at Lisa and ask, "Has anyone told Megan? If she knows already, I'll call her, but if she doesn't know. I think we should just wait."

"We only called you and Matthew's father," Lisa informs me.

"Good. Thank you, Lisa."

We turn as a nurse walks up. "Honey Mitchell?"

"Yes, I'm here." I step forward.

"Matthew is asking for you. If you'll follow me?"

I follow her back to the curtained space. She pulls aside the drape, and I see a pale Matthew sitting up in the hospital bed.

I rush forward. "Matthew. Are you okay?"

His eyes look glassy as he answers, "Yeah, I fell out of the tree house. It really hurt at first." He then grins. "It doesn't hurt that much anymore 'cause they gave me a shot with a needle."

I approach his bed carefully, lean forward, and hug him very gently.

"I heard you were very brave, kiddo," I whisper in his ear.

He gives me a lopsided grin. "I broke my arm. I have a cast. See?" He states with childish pride. "You can sign it later. Dad said he'd get me some markers so everybody in my class can write on it."

I smile down at him. Then I lean over and lovingly smooth his hair off his forehead.

He glances at me wide-eyed. "Holy smokes, Honey. You look beautiful. Doesn't she, Dad?"

"Yes, she does, son. Beautiful," Michael's voice sounds a little gruff.

I can feel the heat of the blush as it spreads over my face.

"Thanks, Matthew," I murmur to the boy.

The doctor comes in and talks to Michael about the fracture. "You could probably take him home, but there was some swelling. So, I think it best if we keep him overnight, just as a precaution." He gives Michael a reassuring smile. "We should be able to release him tomorrow."

Michael's eyes dart to Matthew. "You hear that, Matt? You'll be spending the night here. I can stay with you—"

"Nah, Dad, that's okay," Matthew says with a brave lift of his chin. "Jimmy broke his leg, and he stayed in the hospital all by himself." He slightly slurs his words at the end. It appears the shot they gave him is doing its job.

"You sure?" Michael asks with a frown.

The doctor turns toward us. "We have Matthew highly medicated. He'll probably be asleep soon; we won't even be transferring him to a room. We expect him to sleep through the night. He shouldn't be in any pain right now."

Michael states, "Okay. Thank you, Doctor. I'll return early tomorrow morning."

The doctor nods, and we kiss a sleepy Matthew, whose head is already nodding, and walk back to the waiting room.

"Thanks for waiting," Michael says, then brings Lisa and her husband up to date. "Matthew fractured his arm. He's in a cast. They want to keep him overnight due to some swelling, but I should be able to take him home first thing tomorrow."

Lisa's shoulders slump in relief. "Oh, good. I'm so sorry this happened," she says in a voice filled with guilt. "The kids love playing in that tree house."

Michael shrugs. "I'm a parent. These things happen."

As Michael starts to turn away. "Michael, is it? I'm John, Lisa's husband." John holds out his hand. After they shake, John says, "Hey, you have something on your chin."

Michael frowns, so I get a tissue out of my purse. I reach out and silently wipe the red smear of lipstick off his jaw. I turn the tissue so everyone can see the bright red lipstick.

I feel John and Lisa's eyes go to my sand-colored outfit and then to my nude-colored lip gloss. I smile in grim satisfaction as the other couple realize that the lipstick is not mine.

John states in an uncomfortable voice, "Oh, well... Nice to meet you... Honey, Michael. We'll be leaving now. Sorry, this happened."

We watch as the couple turns and exits the waiting room.

Michael lets out a weary sigh. "Come on, let's go. Matthew is probably already asleep." As we walk toward the car, he murmurs, "Thank God he's alright. A broken bone... I can't forget to buy those markers."

It's a silent ride home. Now that Matthew is out of danger, my thoughts turn to the red lipstick I wiped off Michael's jaw. I press my lips together in a frown. Since when did he start dating? Was it an actual date or just a random hookup in a bar? I don't understand the way I'm feeling, my emotions... I don't have the right to be angry with Michael.

Then I frown as I remember the way Colton reacted at dinner when I got the call about Matthew. I immediately told him I had to leave, and instead of understanding, he put up a fuss. He pulled out a small black velvet box and then issued a warning, "If you leave now, Mary Catherine, we're through."

He crossed his arms as he narrowed his eyes. "I can't have my future wife running off and leaving me to help some older guy with his kids," he demanded in a self-righteous tone.

I gave him a stunned look. "Your future wife? We've only been dating a couple of months—"

"I told you tonight was special," he insisted in a grim voice. "I was going to ask you to marry me."

I rolled my eyes at his tone. "I really don't have time for this." I gave him a direct look. "No, thank you, Colton. It's too soon for a proposal anyway." I impatiently stood. "Now, I need to leave and get to Matthew."

His eyes widen in shocked disbelief. "You're still leaving?"

"Yes. I'm leaving. I love those children," I stated firmly.

"You've got to be kidding! They aren't even yours," he pointed out with a sneer. "You're picking them over me?"

I didn't even answer him. I just hurried out of the restaurant and went to the lobby to call a cab. That's when I ran into Michael.

Michael, who was in a hotel bar— and had red lipstick on his jaw!

The man that I thought was still grieving for his wife! How long has he been dating?

I think back over the last couple of weeks when I thought he was working late at the office. Was he out with another woman, instead?

I try to talk myself out of my rage. He's not mine. He never has been. I'm only the nanny. He pays me to care for his children, cook their food, do their laundry, and clean the house. I'm more like a glorified housekeeper.

I turn to look out the window as I question my feelings. Why do I feel so betrayed by his actions?

I sit there fuming as he silently drives to the house.

Eight

Michael

I can feel the anger as it comes off Honey in waves. I'm not quite sure what she's so mad about. It sounds like her date gave her an ultimatum. That's probably why she's so angry.

I smile in satisfaction. I know Honey will always pick the welfare of my children over someone she's only been dating for a couple of months.

I suddenly sober as I think about Colton calling her his fiancée. Was she actually thinking of marrying that jerk? She said, 'No, thank you,' but what would have happened if Matthew hadn't been injured? A surge of annoyance runs through me at the thought of Honey even dating a guy like that. He was obviously only interested in one thing.

We get to the house, but now we both seem to be in a foul mood. I grimly open the car door for her and notice her struggle to get out of the car gracefully in her snug outfit. I reach in and offer her my hand so she can exit the car.

"Thank you," she murmurs, avoiding my eyes.

"I figured you'd need help since your dress is so tight." Honey hisses in a breath at my mild insult but otherwise remains silent.

I unlock the front door and hold it open for her to pass through into the foyer.

"Yes, I'm sure the person who was wearing the red lipstick had on a similar outfit," I hear the sharp bite in her tone of voice, and it feels like a slap on the face.

"Yes, she did. But her dress didn't quite scream fuck me as loud as yours," the angry words burst from my lips without me thinking them through.

Honey gives a shocked gasp at my crude comment. She then stiffly turns to face me. "What did you just say?" I watch as her eyes flash with fire. "I can't believe you said that to me! How dare you?"

"Well, it's true, isn't it? You were hoping for some action from what's his name?" I fire back.

She crosses her arms and states in a furious tone, "Colton. His name is Colton, and actually, I wasn't." She then hisses, "I don't think of him that way!"

"Why would you continue to date someone for that long if you weren't thinking about sleeping with him? Instead, you were just leading him on?" I clench my jaw as I look down at her in disapproval. "Is that what you like to do? Are you a tease, Honey? Do you tempt men and then leave them hanging?"

"A tease? Are you kidding? I'm here alone every night, caring for your children." She points an accusing finger at me. "You're the one who was out carousing with some, some floozy tonight."

We're both saying things we don't truly mean. I know the type of person Honey is. She isn't any of the things that I'm accusing her of. What the fuck is wrong with me tonight?

My glance lands on her, and I see her lush breasts are heaving with her anger. They're in danger of slipping out of her barely-there dress. Fuck! I shouldn't have looked at her because

EIGHT

now my body has instantly hardened. I burn with an almost primal need. I'm filled with a desire so strong that it threatens to consume me.

I suddenly can't resist my need for Honey any longer. She's too tempting. I reach for her. I push her roughly back against the foyer wall. My hand comes out, and I grab a fistful of her shimmering golden hair. I pull her head back until her wide, startled eyes meet mine.

I growl, "Is this what you want Honey?" Then I'm suddenly devouring her lips. I feel them quiver under my rough assault. Then I feel her surrender, and she opens her mouth to me. I can't get enough. She's going straight to my head—Like a drug.

I'm tall, and even with her heels on, she barely reaches the top of my shoulders. I lean down and cup her lush bottom with my hands. I pull her up against me so she can feel my body's urgent reaction to her. I hear her gasp as she feels my rock-hard response. She then purposely rubs herself against me. I harden even more. A groan slips from my lips.

Honey reaches up and grabs my hair as well. She pulls me back down for her kiss. I feel the slight sting. She's a tigress in my arms. Then I smile more like a lioness with her hair and coloring. I use my hips to pin her against the wall as I let go of her firm ass.

Then I'm reaching into her dress to cup a breast. I feel her nipple pebble at my touch. I rub my wide thumb over it again. It puckers more. I lean down and take it into my mouth. I use my teeth to caress her lightly. She moves against me restlessly.

I feel her press her legs together. I smile in male satisfaction as I reach down to explore her heat. I pull up her dress with one hand and slip my hand into her panties to cover her warm core. She's damp with her arousal. I feel a thrill of masculine triumph, knowing she wants me as much as I want her.

I push into her wet heat with a blunt finger. I test to see how ready she is for me. She bucks against my probing hand. I insert another digit. In and out, I pump into her moistness. Deeper. I'm knuckle-deep. Faster. I don't let up. I increase the tempo. I feel the first flutter, and as I relentlessly continue, she finally shatters uncontrollably in my arms.

"Michael..." She moans my name. I feel her tug on my hair demandingly.

I effortlessly hold her up as I slip her panties down her legs and off of her. Then I unzip my pants, and my hard cock springs free. I'm big. I slide her up against the hard wall, and then, with my hands around her hips, I guide her onto my thick erection. I enter her as slowly as I can to try and give her body time to adjust to my girth and length.

I hear her gasp, and then she raises her legs and wraps them around me. That changes the angle, and I pound into her again and again. I hope I'm not hurting her as I roughly pin her against the unyielding wall. I can't stop. I continue to surge into her as I take her, each thrust harder and faster than the one before.

The wall shakes, and I hear a picture as it falls to the floor, but we hardly notice. It doesn't interrupt us. Our need for each other is out of control. It's too intense. I've never felt this type of consuming desire before.

I feel her body tighten around me as she yells my name loudly. I can only grunt at her response. Then she's milking me as my balls tighten close to my body, and I follow her in the most intense release I've ever felt.

It's finally over. I loosen my hold until she can slide down the wall. I support her as she finds her balance on wobbly legs.

We stand there exhausted and in shock at our actions. I feel like the months before were just foreplay, and this is the culmination of what I've been feeling for her for quite a while.

I shut my eyes, then open them and look down at her. She's my kids' nanny. Honey is off-limits! They need her. I'm her boss, for Christ's sake. I pay her salary! I feel a wrenching knot form in my gut... What have I done? Have I ruined everything?

"I'm... I'm so sorry, Honey. I... this should never have happened," I stammer as I push her away from me. I can't believe what I just allowed to happen.

She glances up at me and whispers, "Michael—" But I avoid her eyes.

"No, no. It was my fault. Honey, again, I'm sorry." I hear the remorse in my voice. "This should not have happened. It was a mistake." I steel my resolve as I grind out, "It won't happen again. I promise."

I finally let go of her arms, then turn and walk doggedly upstairs... into the room I shared with my late wife.

I let out a ragged sigh in disbelief at my uncontrollable actions. Then, with a shake of my head, I make a vow. I will not allow myself to physically lose control like that again.

I walk over and pick up my wife's picture with shaking hands. I turn and carefully place it in the closet. In the same box where I have the purse, she carried during our wedding.

EIGHT

I stand there waiting for the guilt to hit me... but it doesn't. Shouldn't I feel like I've betrayed my wife? No. I shut my eyes as a memory surfaces... Michelle made it clear before she passed that she released me from our vows. In fact, she made me promise her that I would someday find someone else to care about. At the time, I didn't appreciate her sentiment. It actually made me angry.

I wearily shake my head. My only vow now is never to allow myself to love that deeply. Losing Michelle broke me. I can't allow any woman ever to get that close again.

I numbly take off my clothes and step into the shower. I let the hot water run over me. I try not to think about what just happened. I resolutely keep my mind empty of all thoughts. It's a trick I learned after Michelle died.

I wearily crawl into bed. Naked. I close my eyes, and even though I thought I'd never be able to sleep, my body is exhausted, and I fall into a restless sleep.

Nine

Honey

I watch in stunned disbelief as Michael slowly walks away. I look around in a daze. I see the picture that the force of our lovemaking knocked off the wall. I go over, pick it up, and hang it in place. It's a collage of the children. I turn my eyes away once it's hanging straight again.

I look around the foyer. It looks the same as always. Why should it look different just because I feel different? Suddenly, my legs don't want to support me. I sit down on the bench that is normally reserved for the children's backpacks. I lean back and take a shaky breath.

NINE

I just had sex with Michael. The man I've worked for the last two years. My employer. How will we ever be able to have a normal working relationship again? We see each other every single day. Multiple times a day.

How am I supposed to act around him going forward? Now that I know how hot his lovemaking is, how he feels inside me. How his hands, his mouth felt on my breast. I'm breathless, just thinking of how he took me so roughly against the wall. He was so forceful; he was such a demanding lover.

My smile dims. I've wondered about his lovemaking. Heck, I've dreamed about his lovemaking. He asked me why I kept going out with Colton when I didn't think about my date that way. I wonder what Michael would have said if I had told him the truth. I kept going out with Colton as a cover so that no one would suspect I'd fallen in love with my boss.

Yes, that's me. I tried so hard not to. I mean, who wants to be in love with a man who doesn't even notice them? I sigh and defeatedly rest my head back against the wall.

How could I not fall in love with Michael? He's everything I've ever wanted in a man, a husband. He's thoughtful, nice, and he's mature. He's a gentleman. He holds the door open for me... and I've daydreamed about him since the day I met him.

I knew he was still grieving over the death of his wife. Even that impressed me. He loved his wife. He's been loyal. Even in death, he continues to cherish her. He's done such a great job as a single dad. The way he loves those kids. He's patient and kind, yet stern when he needs to be. Oh man, even I know I sound like a love-sick teenager.

About six months after being hired, I realized that I had fallen hopelessly in love with Michael. I thought I could hide it. I started going out on dates. I even tried to will myself to fall in love with Colton, but he was nothing like Michael. Not even close.

And all those daydreams about my employer? Ha! They didn't hold a candle to reality and to what his lovemaking felt like tonight. It was so hot, so rough, so wonderful. I close my eyes as another sigh escapes my lips.

I finally raise my head and give myself a stern pep talk. I can get through this, for the children's sake. I love them too much to quit just because their father doesn't want a relationship with me. I still respect the man. I still love him, only now... I know how it feels to be taken by him... I just hope I can hide my attraction. The longing I feel to be held in his arms.

NINE

It was easier before when I only had my dreams. My imagination. Now that I've actually had a taste of what could be? Please don't let me embarrass myself around him!

I sit there for another minute, lost in thoughts of what could be... until I finally roust myself and stand up. I pick up my abandoned panties off the floor, and with my head held high, I enter my apartment. Then I turn and flip the deadbolt to lock the door. I grimly laugh at the lock as I realize I'm locking myself in and not Michael out.

I take a hot shower, pull on a nightgown, and crawl into my bed. A shiver runs down my spine as I think of Michael alone in the house.

The familiar sound of a night owl outside my window echoes through the quiet night. It sounds as lonely as I feel.

I pull the covers up tighter around me, but the warmth can't dispel the chill that settles in my bones. I roll over, hugging the pillow to my chest, and try to ignore the heavy weight I feel in my chest. The thought of facing Michael so soon after what happened between us fills me with dread. I close my eyes, wishing I could simply disappear.

Taking a deep breath, I force myself to focus on the children. I can't let my feelings for their father ruin my relationship with them. They love me, and I love them. This isn't their fault. It isn't Michael's fault... No. It's my fault...

I don't remember falling asleep, but suddenly, it's morning, and the alarm clock's insistent beeping pierces the silence. I groan and roll over, silencing the obnoxious noise. There's no need to get up early. Michael is fully capable of making his own breakfast and I'm not ready to face him yet.

I determinedly turn my thoughts away from Micheal and think instead of his son.

Matthew won't be released until after nine, and Megan isn't due home until the afternoon. I run through my mental checklist of chores. I guess I won't be taking Matthew to get his haircut today.

I suddenly grin in relief as I get an idea. I know what will raise Matthew's spirits!

I jump out of bed, eager to put my plan into action. Dressing quickly, I grab my keys and head to the grocery store. I fill my cart with all of Matthew's favorite foods, then add a rainbow of permanent markers. Michael might have already bought some, but it can't hurt to have extras.

I then ask the florist department to fill up some balloons. I even pick up a small cake. So, what if I want to take this opportunity

NINE

to spoil Matthew? He was so brave after breaking his arm and having to stay overnight in the hospital that he deserves a little celebration. I take all my packages to the car and drive home. I bring everything in and spend a few minutes decorating the dining room.

I even take a couple of the balloons up to Matthew's bedroom. He's growing up so fast. His room used to be filled with fire trucks, spiderman, and dinosaurs, but now he has anime, avatars, and gaming paraphernalia.

I walk downstairs as it's almost ten o'clock. Michael and Matthew should be arriving any minute. I get out the blender, and I make a chocolate malt milkshake. I hear the door open right as I finish. I turn around and see Matthew as he walks in.

His eyes light up as he sees the balloons and then the chocolate cake on the table.

"Cool! Thanks, Honey." As he comes closer, I give him a warm hug.

I find a tall glass and a straw for his malt. He sits down at the head of the table as his father walks in.

Matthew looks up with a delighted grin and says, "Look, Dad, I feel like it's my birthday. Honey decorated."

Michael smiles and says easily, "I see that. Thank you, Honey."

I can only nod at Michael as I don't trust my voice right now.

Michael takes out a small, clear bag of prescription medicine and hands it to me. "Matthew should only get these if he's in any pain. They help reduce the ache and prevent inflammation."

I swallow, my heart pounding in my chest. My hands tremble slightly as I take the medication bag. It's as difficult as I thought it would be to face Michael today.

"Dad, Honey, will you both sign my cast?" Matthew asks as he looks up hopefully.

"Absolutely," I assure him.

We both sit on either side of Matthew. Michael picks up a bright red marker and writes Dad in his flowing scrawl. I pick up different colors and write out Honey with each letter in a different color.

Once we're done, Matthew looks proudly down at his signed cast. "Cool, I can't wait to show the other kids in my class."

I dish out a slice of cake for each of us, and then Matthew is off to play with his games. I glance briefly over at Michael, who is careful not to look at me. He gets up from the table, steps into his home office, and quietly closes the door.

I clear the table and try to stay out of Michael's way for the rest of the morning by doing odd chores around the house. As I decide to clean and organize the pantry, I have a hard time keeping my thoughts on the task at hand. My mind keeps returning to what it felt like to be held in Michael's strong arms.

Ten

Michael

It's almost lunchtime, and I've stayed away as long as I intend to. Enough! So what? We lost control and had sex. It's over. It's done. We got it out of our system... Yeah, right. My lips twist into a grimace. Who am I trying to convince?

My stomach growls as I missed breakfast and that one small slice of cake did nothing to satisfy my hunger. I'm ready for some good food. It's now or never. I hear Honey call Matthew down for lunch. I walk slowly into the dining room as I brace myself to get through this. We have to move on, or there will always be an elephant in the room, and I can't have this type of awkwardness between us.

TEN

I sit down at the table, ready for a hearty meal. Instead, I see macaroni and cheese and beanie weenies? I can't help but laugh. Trust Honey to make Matthew feel extra special. She's been wonderful to my kids. I couldn't ask for a more caring and thoughtful person to be here for my children.

I meet her eyes. "Thank you, Honey," I tell her sincerely. "I love what you do for this family."

I see her eyes widen, and then she gives me a small smile. "I like children, and yours are my favorite."

I let out a bark of laughter as Matthew comes in. He gives a joyful whoop when he sees his favorite foods on the table and sits down to dig in. Honey and I exchange a silent grin. The ice has been broken, and it almost feels like things are back to normal between us again.

It feels like a very long weekend. I can't be blamed if my eyes unconsciously follow Honey as she goes about her daily tasks. When she stands on her tiptoes to reach something high in the cabinets, her shirt reveals her taunt, bare mid-drift, and I have to drag my eyes away.

So what? Maybe soon, my mind will stop hearing her voice as it cried out my name as she came in my arms. I wearily run my fingers through my hair as I quote, 'This too shall pass,' silently in my head.

When Megan returns home, Matthew tells her all about his ordeal. How he fell out of the treehouse, stayed at the hospital overnight by himself, and how the doctor put the cast on his arm. I'm proud of my daughter, who let him tell her without once rolling her eyes.

Megan can be patient with her brother when she wants to be. She's a great older sister.

I'm back at the corporate office bright and early Monday morning. I see Jeff in the breakroom.

"How's your son?"

"He has a fracture. They put his arm in a cast. Right now, he's more excited about having all his classmates sign his cast than anything else."

"Good. I'm glad he's okay." He grins as he informs me, "Colleen was disappointed that you guys didn't get to hook up."

TEN

I shrug and keep on walking; I don't feel like talking about Colleen this morning. Unfortunately, I may be seeing more of her as she's remotely involved with my new case. Once I reach my office, I buzz my admin. "Nancy, could you bring me the file on that potential case? Also, call my team and set up a meeting after lunch, please."

I look up when Nancy drops off the file. I immediately begin reading through my notes. I can't seem to shake the bad feeling I get as I double-check everything. What about this case has me constantly looking over my shoulder?

It's a busy day, yet at odd moments, images of Honey invade my thoughts. The way her eyes darken to a deeper brown with her emotions. The way her smile can brighten a room. She was like a breath of fresh air when she first came into our lives. I've thanked Trent a thousand times for submitting her resume.

I can't help but smile as I remember the day Honey first joined our family. She had a way of calming even the most chaotic of situations. Like the time, Matthew and Megan were arguing over the remote control. With a few well-chosen words, she turned their bickering into a game of rock-paper-scissors.

She always kept our family outings organized and fun. I think back to the summer camping trip spent in an RV and how I slept with Matthew, and she and Megan took the double bed.

I think of how Honey looked in her swimsuit when we went tubing down the river.

I think of the hundreds of times I noticed her lush, curvy body yet never once allowed myself to dwell on my attraction to her. Instead, I would resolutely push any thoughts of Honey as a woman out of my head. I never wanted to lose the normality she brought to my family—the feeling of being a family unit again.

To me, Honey must be off-limits. A sigh escapes my lips as I wearily rub my hands over my face. It's simple. I can't lose Honey. She's a great nanny. She's important to my family, my children...and to me.

It's all the countless thoughtful little things she does for each of us. I love it when she surprises me with an apple pie just because it's my favorite. She decorated the house with balloons for Matthew and how she helps Megan with cheerleading and assists at their schools. Yes, she gets paid for all that. But no other person, no matter how much I paid them, will ever care about us like Honey does.

A wave of realization hits me as I continue reminiscing about my life and my family—not once have I thought about Michelle. I feel like a weight has been lifted from my shoulders. In a way that is uniquely her, Honey has filled our home with warmth, laughter, and love. Somehow, without diminishing our love for Michelle, she helped heal our wounds of loss.

That night, I arrive home late. I called Honey earlier to tell her I wouldn't be making it home for dinner. I quietly let myself in the house and make my way to the kitchen. I open the fridge, and there's a covered plate. I pull it out and place it in the microwave.

After it's warmed, I sit down and take a bite. It's good. Honey is a good cook. She's not fancy, but her roasts always melt in your mouth, and her mashed potatoes are delicious. I notice she put extra gravy in my dish because she knows that's what I prefer.

I ruefully shake my head as I would rather have blue balls forever than jeopardize our current family unit, and that includes Honey.

I hear a noise and glance up to see her standing silently by the door. Her hair is tousled, and she has on a silky nightgown beneath her thin robe. Her slender feet are bare.

In a voice just above a whisper, she says, "I'm sorry, I didn't know you were down here. I just came in to get one of the cookies I made earlier."

I meet her eyes. "Come and join me, Honey." When she doesn't move, I add, "Please?"

I hear her sigh, and then she gets a cookie and a glass of cold milk and sits down across from me.

"That's better. Look... about what happened. I can never apologize enough, but I want to put it behind us. Remember when we used to meet like this after the kids were in bed? It was... comfortable. Safe." I give her an earnest look. "I... I don't want to lose this, Honey. What we have without the sexual attraction is too precious to me."

After my little speech, Honey remains silent, looking down at her hands.

"Well, Honey? Can we try to get things back to normal?" I ask her, "Can we forget about what happened that night? Do you think we can do that?"

She gives me a grateful smile with just a trace of sadness. "Yes, Michael. I think I'd like that," she finally says in a soft voice.

I reach out, wanting to give her a comforting pat on the hand... but decide it's better if I don't. Instead, I give her a sheepish smile.

"Good. That's all I ask." As our eyes meet, I say, "Thank you."

TEN

We remain sitting there for a few moments, and the silence feels natural, not strained. Honey eats her cookie, and I eat my dinner.

With a smile, I glance at her again—and notice there's a crumb on her lip... I immediately want to kiss it off. Shit! I try not to let her see me looking at her lips as I dart my eyes away.

Dammit. I've got to do better than this! Honey silently gets up, rinses out her glass, and sets it in the sink. She nods, smiles, then pads softly out of the kitchen. I look down at my hand wrapped tightly around my fork and try to ignore the hardness of my body's instant response to her softness.

We've got to make this work. Maybe I should start dating other women. But then I scowl. I don't want anyone else! If I can't have Honey, then I'd rather be alone.

Eleven

Honey

No! This can't be happening! I close my eyes, then blink them open and look again. The two pink lines are still there.

I've been getting slightly nauseous in the mornings, but I thought it was just allergies. Then, this morning, I threw up my breakfast. It startled me into awareness.

I checked the calendar and realized that I had missed my monthly cycles. I'm irregular, so I wasn't that concerned at first. I decided to take a pregnancy test just to put my mind at ease.

Ha! I look down at the two pink lines and suddenly feel queasy again.

How did this happen? Then I start to laugh. I know how this happened; it happened so fast that we didn't use protection.

I lean heavily against the bathroom counter. This pregnancy would change everything. I have to be sure before I say anything to Michael.

A desperate thought flows through my mind—I could just leave and never tell anyone…but then I frown. I can't do that! I could never just leave these kids. I wouldn't do that! But what will Michael want to do?

I remember the censure in Lisa's husband's eyes. There will be more talk and rumors. It's not scandalous to have a baby out of wedlock…but… It all feels so complicated!

I put my hand protectively over my abdomen. I'm pro-choice, but my decision would always be to have the baby.

A baby. I'm a mother! I feel a small thrill inside of me. The way I love children, I could never think of conceiving as anything more than a miracle and blessing. I send a wave of pure love to the tiny seed of life growing inside of me as a soft smile covers my face.

I glance in the mirror. My eyes look bright and filled with a wondrous joy. A wide smile spreads across my reflection. First things first... I have to confirm that I'm pregnant. You always hear stories about home kits being wrong. I call my doctor and ask for the next available appointment.

Tomorrow at one thirty. That time is perfect, as I'll be out in plenty of time to pick up the kids from school, and no one has to be the wiser.

I shakily look down at the pamphlets clutched in my hand. My doctor gave them to me after she confirmed that I was pregnant. She was wonderful and answered all of my questions. However, I'm still reeling from the shocking news.

Pregnant. There's a tiny life inside of me, growing. As a sliver of dread creeps into my awareness, I sternly remind myself that I've always wanted to be a mother.

I ruefully grimace because, in my daydreams, I imagined things happening in a specific order. First, the man would declare his undying love for me and propose. Next, there would be my dream wedding, and then, and only then... in fact, maybe a couple of years down the road... only then would we plan for a family—a baby.

I glance at the car clock. I better get moving. I still need to pick up Matthew and Megan. I put the car in drive as I push my thoughts to the back of my mind. I'll have more time to think about this later, once everyone is in bed and I'm alone. I put the pamphlets in the bottom of my purse.

I pick up Matthew first, and he rambles on about class and their pet rat in a cage.

When Megan climbs into the car, I ask, "How was your day?"

"It was okay, but there's this girl named Cathy, she is so mean. I don't want to be in her silly group anyway," but I can see the longing in her eyes.

"Geez, Megan, all girls are mean! Who cares?" Matthew shrugs. "Just ignore her. Duh."

"What do you know? Not all girls are mean!" Then, with her famous eye roll. "You're just a stupid boy!"

I listen to them chatter back and forth. It's the same as most other days, except now I'm carrying a baby inside of me. A child. I smile secretly to myself as I continue to listen to the kids as I drive.

They unload their backpacks on the front bench, and we continue to the kitchen.

"Milk and cookies? There's chocolate chip," I ask with a grin.

Matthew instantly answers me. "Yeah, and a big glass of milk."

I pour them each a glass and put out the cookies, which they devour as their after-school snack.

I arch an eyebrow at them. "How about spaghetti and meatballs for dinner?"

Megan answers this time. "Sure, with lots of garlic bread."

"And chocolate cake?" Matthew adds.

"Finish your homework, and you can have chocolate cake for dessert, Matt."

Later, as the pasta water boils, I find myself daydreaming about holding a sweet little bundle of joy. While I am confident with children, I have absolutely no experience with an infant. Zero. Zilch. It's a little daunting. I then think about my family. How will my father and my grandpa react? I wince.

I close my eyes. I send up a silent prayer, open my eyes, and start to set the table. It's almost time for Michael to get home. I have no idea how I'm going to break the news to him. But he's the father, and he needs to know. I ignore the knot tightening in my chest.

I try to imagine what our child will look like. I'm sure it will resemble Megan and Matthew. But what color eyes will it have? I give a dreamy little smile.

It's after six o'clock. Michael hasn't called, and I don't want supper to get cold, so I call the children to dinner.

"Megan! Matt! Time to eat," I hear their footsteps stomp down the stairs.

"Where's Dad?" Megan asks curiously.

"I'm not sure. I haven't heard from him." I state with a shrug, "He's probably just running a little late."

I dish up their plates. Then I sit down and fix a plate for me.

"I still don't like algebra," Megan informs us as she takes a bite of spaghetti.

"Yeah, math sucks." Matthew agrees. "My favorite class is gym. We ran relay races today! It was fun," he informs us, his eyes bright with excitement.

I listen to the children as they talk about what they did in school that day. They are always so full of energy. My thoughts again drift to the baby and Michael...

Soon, we've cleaned our plates.

"Your dad must be running late. Why don't you help me clear the table and put everything in the dishwasher?"

Megan lifts her chin and states, "Sure, but Matt puts them in the dishwasher wrong."

Matthew frowns at his sister. "I do not!" Then he shrugs. "Fine, do it by yourself then."

"No, you just need to learn how to do it right," Megan says, looking down her nose at him.

I give both of them a stern look and ask, "Megan, Matt, would you rather wash them by hand?"

Both kids look at me in horror.

"What?"

"No! Of course not."

"Well, when I was growing up, we sometimes had to wash the dishes by hand."

ELEVEN

Matthew grimaces and asks, "Geez, when did you have to wash them by hand?"

"When my father got tired of listening to us kids argue and complain," I answer dryly.

Silence. Then, Megan sighs. "Fine, I'll load the dishwasher, but Matt has to clear the table."

"I'd rather clear the table, anyway," he tells her.

I try not to smile at their effort to be agreeable. They finish their chores in relative silence.

"We're done." Both of them turn to me.

I smile at them. "Great. Let's make up a plate for your father."

"Okay." Megan helps me fix a covered plate for Michael. I tell her, "Go ahead and put it in the fridge. I'm sure he'll be home soon."

As I glance again at the clock, I feel a hint of unease as Michael always calls me whenever he's running late. I hope everything is okay. I would feel a little silly if I called him to find out he was already on his way home.

After seven o'clock, I finally give in to my worry and call Michael.

An unknown woman's voice answers, "Michael Garret's phone."

"Is Michael there?" I ask.

"Not right at the moment. He'll be back soon, though," she advises me. "May I take a message?"

"No, thank you." I hang up the phone.

Was that the red lipstick lady? My heart sinks. Did our time together mean nothing to him? Does he even care about me at all?... Tonight, I was going to tell Michael about our baby... but I don't want to have that conversation with him if he's been with *her*.

I feel the sting of tears burn my eyes. I sit there for a few minutes, just staring blindly at the phone, hoping that Michael will call me right back... willing the phone to ring.

It remains silent. A wave of disappointment washes over me as I force a smile. Of course, he's busy. I tell myself, trying to convince my anxious mind. But deep down, I can't shake the feeling that something's off.

The kids are watching their favorite TV show. I reluctantly drag myself over and join them on the couch.

"When will Dad be home?" Matthew asks me during a commercial.

"I'm not sure. He's probably working on a case and just forgot to let me know." I shrug as if I'm unconcerned.

When it's the children's bedtime, I turn off the lights, and instead of staying up worrying, I decide to go to bed myself.

I want to listen for Michael to come home so I will myself to stay awake. Instead, I fall fast asleep the minute I shut my eyes, but my dreams are restless and frightening.

I roll over and cover my head when my alarm goes off the next morning. When I finally crawl out of bed, my eyelids feel heavy, like I didn't even sleep. I glance at my phone but don't see a text or call from Michael. I wonder when he got home last night. Surely, he wouldn't stay out all night without calling.

I spend a few minutes getting sick in the bathroom. Then I wearily get dressed and walk into the kitchen. I hear Megan and Matthew upstairs. Soon, they come bounding down the steps as I set out their cereal.

"Where's Dad? Is he still sleeping?" Matthew asks.

"Looks that way," I say noncommittally.

I drop Megan and Matthew off at their schools and then sit in the car, wondering if I should return to the house or not. I shake my head silently in defeat, as where else would I go? I drive home to fix a cup of hot tea and some dry toast. Then, after I tidy up the kitchen, I head to my apartment.

Twelve

Michael

It's been a rough night. I glance at my watch and wince. It's past three in the morning. I have no idea what Honey and the kids are thinking. I always let them know if I'm going to be late. And I always come home at night. I wonder if Honey has jumped to the wrong conclusion, but then I scrunch my shoulders in a shrug. After we agreed that night together was a mistake, she probably thought I was out carousing. It's probably for the best, I decide with a grim twist of my lips.

My hands tighten on the steering wheel as I think back over the events of the past twenty-four hours. I had wondered what Colleen's motives were, what she truly wanted from me. I had a feeling it wasn't just about sex. Boy, was I right. She finally came into the office, sat down, and propositioned me.

No, not for sex. That would have been too easy. Instead, she leaned forward, her eyes glinting with a mix of menace and promise. "I have a proposition for you, Michael," she said, her voice low and seductive. "A very lucrative one."

She explained her offer, her voice dripping with the promise of wealth and power. I felt a shiver run down my spine. Colleen's clients are heavily involved with the mob. She's on a retainer to represent their... I'll call them 'employees' of some of the most feared members of the mob syndicate. She is paid to ensure those 'employees' get off with no or moderate sentences.

If one of her clients ever wanted to plea bargain based on their inner knowledge of the organization, I have a feeling they wouldn't ever make it to trial. Colleen is working for some very dangerous clientele. Clients who will permanently silence anyone they believe is a threat.

The people who were sent to talk to me last night strongly suggested I not call anyone. When Colleen calmly handed me back my phone this morning, I noticed that Honey had called twice. She didn't leave a voicemail. But I'm already on my way home.

TWELVE

I grimace as my mind goes again to what transpired earlier. These same people who confiscated my cell phone want me to represent one of their own at the last minute. They laughed when I argued that I have a family and don't want any connections to their organization.

They had seen how I handled a similar murder case for a man named Frank Zappo. It was about five years ago, and I had no idea my client had connections with the mob until I was already deeply involved in the case.

I let my mind go back to that time...

Days had turned into weeks as the murder case dragged on. The evidence against Frank Zappo, my client, was overwhelming.

I remember sitting in my office, a stack of files on my desk. My phone rings. It's my investigator calling to tell me he's found something. My heart pounded with apprehension as I hung up the phone. I knew Frank Zappo was involved in something shady, but I never expected to find out he was in bed with the mob.

My team and I kept digging and digging, turning over every rock. Finally, at the last minute, we came across evidence pointing to the true guilty party.

When I was able to point the finger at the correct culprit, there was a lot of press coverage. At the time, I was just glad it was all over. I couldn't wait to walk away. I didn't want to owe anyone a favor, especially with the crowd that my client ran with, and I truly didn't want them to be beholden to me. My family's safety always comes first.

I made sure that all ties were severed. And they were until that previous client, Frank Zappo, turned up dead, and now the accused suspect wants me and only me to represent him. And the suspect, who is my would-be client? Oh yeah, it just gets better and better. He's Victor Mazarano. Son of Vito Mazarano. Which means I would be working for the head of one of the most feared mobsters. Great. Just great.

I tried very hard to turn them down. I couldn't understand why they wanted me when they already had Colleen on retainer. However, this client normally gets what and who he wants. So, by the end of the night, I was 'strongly' advised to accept the offer to take over representing Victor Mazarano. I have to give them my answer by the end of the week.

I give a huge yawn. I'm tired. I need to sleep, yet I already feel the strain of having to exonerate him. I spent last night going over every aspect of his case so far, and the bottom line is—It doesn't look good.

TWELVE

I shake my head. Right now. I just want to get home and sleep for a week.

When I pull into the driveway, I wearily get out of the car and go inside. I trudge upstairs to my bedroom, undress, and fall into bed. I'm totally exhausted. I'm asleep before my head hits the pillow.

I groggily open my eyes and see sunlight. I blink as I sit up and slide my legs over the side of the bed. I look at the clock. It's eleven thirty. I've slept for over eight hours straight. I stretch as I get up and take a shower. I throw on some jeans and a T-shirt and go downstairs in my bare feet.

I glance around, but the kids are long gone. They left for school hours ago.

I open the refrigerator and see a covered plate. I open it up. It's cold spaghetti and meatballs. I'm standing there holding the leftovers when Honey walks into the kitchen.

She asks quietly, "Do you want breakfast?"

"Um... yeah. If you don't mind."

Honey removes the eggs and sausage from the fridge and begins fixing me a hot meal. I sit down at the kitchen table and watch as she silently throws everything together in a pan. I hear the sizzle and smell of the fried meat. When it's ready, she puts it all on a plate with a slice of toast and deftly places it in front of me. She gets a fork and a napkin for me as well.

I'm surprised when she doesn't join me. I miss the easy conversations we typically have.

I silently eat my meal, but I keep my eyes on Honey. She doesn't sit down but hasn't left the kitchen either. She's obviously upset. Her shoulders are slumped, and her hands are trembling. I can tell she's trying to gather the courage to confront me. When she blindly swipes a cloth over the same spot on the counter, I determinedly put down my fork and push away my plate.

"Honey, you obviously have something to tell me," I say in a firm voice. "But I already know what you have to say to me."

She glances at me with wide, incredulous eyes. "You do?" She asks in a hesitant voice.

"Yes, I've been married before." I meet her eyes calmly. "I recognize the signs."

TWELVE

I watch as her shoulders slump in relief. "Good. I... I've been thinking about how to tell you," she stammers the words out. "If you already know... It makes this a lot easier." She glances up at me warily. "I thought it was going to be more of a shock."

"No, I'm not even that surprised, really," I say with a rueful twist of my lips. "I take full responsibility, Honey."

"Michael, I'm glad you're being so calm about this." I watch as the worry lines on her face clear.

I reach out and squeeze her hand with a reassuring smile.

She glances up at me ruefully, and I see that her smile is filled with relief as she shakily admits, "I guess since this will be your third, you know what to expect."

"Yes, I... my third?" I frown in confusion. "Wait a minute. My third what?"

Honey's glance turns confused. She says slowly, "Your third child."

"My third child? Honey, what the hell are we talking about?"

She seems as bewildered as I feel. Honey gives me a strange look. "The baby," she says in a low voice.

"What baby?" I ask with a fierce scowl.

Honey's face pales. She looks down at her abdomen, her eyes filling with fear and uncertainty.

"Our baby... the baby I'm carrying," she says, slowly enunciating each word.

I practically shout, "You're pregnant?"

I'm stunned. My mind races as I try to process the information. I sit there, frozen, unable to speak.

Honey's eyes fill with tears. "Michael, why are you shouting? You're acting surprised. You... you said you already knew."

I slump back in my chair and look up at the ceiling. I take a deep breath to try and hold everything together. I don't want to lose my patience or temper with her.

"Honey. I thought you were upset because I didn't call you to let you know I would be late last night."

She raises her chin and narrows her eyes at me.

"Well, yes. I did want to talk to you about the woman who answered your phone." Honey crosses her arms over her chest and says with an edge to her voice, "Especially since I'm pregnant with your child, but when you said you already knew about the baby... I thought you had figured it out."

TWELVE

I pinch the bridge of my nose between my thumb and my forefinger.

"This can't be happening... Not now. This is a nightmare," I whisper to myself.

I hear Honey make a noise. I open my eyes to see her crestfallen face. I watch as tears begin to stream down her face. Her shoulders start to shake as she pulls in a deep breath of air.

"Ah, shit. Honey, don't cry," I reach over and take her hand in mine. "Please. I didn't mean it. Honest."

"So, you're glad about the baby?" She asks with a doubtful glance at me between wet lashes.

"Well, no... but..." I hear her start to cry in earnest.

"Honey, I'm sorry. I know I'm really messing this up." I run my fingers through my hair. "It's just a shock, that's all. I didn't know this could happen—"

She interrupts me with a glare. "Really? You already have two children. You didn't know this was a possibility?"

I can't help it. I start to laugh. "Honey. I meant that I thought you were on the pill or—"

"So, now you think it's my fault?" She jerks her hand away.

"No. No… I don't… truly. Look, let me start over, okay?"

Honey continues to look at me with suspicion as she wipes the tears from her cheeks.

"I didn't know you were trying to tell me that you're pregnant. While it's a shock, we'll get through this. You and I, together." I give her a sincere look and reach out to take her hand again. "No matter what. Alright?"

She gives a hiccupy nod and sniffs, but her eyes are still filled with a lingering wariness.

"As for being glad, I like being a father. You already know that about me. Right?" She nods again solemnly, her eyes studying my face warily.

"When I said it was a nightmare… I meant the timing is off. Last night, well, I will be representing a very unsavory criminal, and I just didn't want to put my family, which includes you and now this baby, in harm's way." I give her a reassuring smile. "I'll explain it all to you later. After I've had time to let this all sink in."

I stand up, go around the table, and lift her bodily from the chair. I sit down and place her on my lap. I wrap my arms comfortingly around her while she leans her head against my chest.

TWELVE

"Listen. I think we should get married. These past few months have been torture. I already think of us as a family. I mean, we've basically been living together for over two years."

I rub her back with a soothing touch as I continue in a slow but steady voice, "Honey, I care about you. I'm also very attracted to you. I didn't want my desire to spoil what we had. But now? Let's go ahead and get married... right away. Okay?"

Thirteen

Honey

I rest there in Michael's arms while he talks to me about getting married. His low voice washes over me. He's already making plans for our future.

"I hope you don't mind a small wedding..." he murmurs softly.

It sounded wonderful when he first suggested marriage, but as he continued talking about it, I noticed that he never once mentioned love. He hasn't told me that he loves me. I feel a lump form in my throat.

I realize the truth... Michael is not in love with me. The blow leaves me feeling winded and bruised.

I know that he cares about me. But caring about someone isn't the same as being in love.

He's a wonderful man and a great father, so of course, he's willing to do the right thing and marry me... because I'm pregnant with his child.

I give a sad little smile as I settle back into his arms while he continues talking.

"I know Megan and Matt will be excited. They will love that we're going to be a true family now," he says quietly.

I take a deep breath as I have an important decision to make. Right now. I can stay with this man and his children and have a good life. But will my love alone be enough? I'm suddenly not sure.

Doubt starts to cloud my mind. I love this man. I am in love with Michael. But what will happen in a few years when he still doesn't return that love? Will I have the courage to walk away? Will I ever be able to walk away from Michael willingly?

I look up at his rugged face. He's wearing a gentle smile as he talks about our family unit. Michael doesn't mention us being a couple, our marriage. He's more focused on our future as a family.

"I wonder if we'll end up having two girls or two boys?" He glances down at me as he asks curiously, "Do you have a preference?"

I shake my head gently at his question, but my internal dialog continues. No. I don't think I'll ever be able to walk away from this man willingly. I sigh as I rest my cheek against Michael's chest and listen to the rhythmic thump of his heart. Suddenly, my thoughts clear, and I know what I'll do.

I'll stay. I'll marry him. I'll take what scraps he throws my way. It won't even be a hardship. These past two years, I've hidden my love for him away and just enjoyed every minute of living with him caring for him and his children. I don't see that ever changing...at least not for me. How pathetic is that?

I reach up and smooth back a lock of Michael's dark hair. He turns and kisses my hand.

I smile and think of my unborn baby. My hand settles lovingly over my still-flat stomach. I know he'll love this baby, just like he loves and cherishes Megan and Matthew. I couldn't ask for a better father. A better man.

Suddenly, I feel a flash of fear. A hard kernel of despair forms like a knot in the pit of my stomach from knowing that Michael may never be able to love me the way I love him. The way he loved Michelle. Can I accept that? Can I bear it? In a few years, will I turn bitter?

He had something so special with Michelle. Maybe I'm destined to forever stand in *her* shadow. Raise *her* children and live with *her* husband.

I look down at my hand that still covers my abdomen. This baby isn't Michelle's. It's mine and Michael's. This baby will make everything bearable. This is our baby. I feel a tiny flicker of hope. Hope for the future.

Michael turns my face to his and gives me a kiss full of longing, even if it's not full of love.

I return his kiss. I raise my hands and run them lovingly through his dark hair.

I know that he wants me, that he desires me. His passion will have to be enough for right now.

His body grows hard beneath me.

"See what you do to me, Honey?" He murmurs hoarsely in my ear.

I purposely rub against him and feel him harden even more.

This I can give him. And if he only longs for my body, if that is all he can give me—then I'll take it.

"Michael, I like the way your chest feels." I run my hands inside his T-shirt. I hear his swift intake of breath as I trace his defined abs. I suddenly tug his shirt over his head and off of him. I take my fingers and skim his broad shoulders, feeling his muscles bunch in response.

He immediately sets me on my feet as he stands. He swiftly pulls off his jeans and briefs.

"Your turn," Michael says huskily as he sits back down on the chair and pulls my sundress over my head. He makes short work of my panties.

"You're not wearing a bra," he murmurs with an appreciative grin. I feel his hands cover my full breasts.

"Come here, Honey." His hands go firmly around my waist as he positions me on his lap, facing him.

His hands and then his mouth caress my breasts. I swear my nipples are already feeling more sensitive. His face is rough as he hasn't shaved yet. I feel the prickle of his beard as he nuzzles against my softer skin.

"I love your lush breasts," he lets out a low groan. "They're so responsive."

I feel them pebble as his warm breath washes over them. He urgently takes one of my hardened nipples into his warm mouth.

As Michael lightly pulls and sucks against me, my hands hold him to me. I ache to have him inside me. I move restlessly on his lap, trying to show him what I want as my throat feels too thick to speak.

His big hands roughly grab my hips, and then he's lifting me effortlessly above him.

"You're so light. Ride me, Honey. I want to be inside you, now," he demands.

He brings me down onto his full erection. I gasp as he fills me, feeling my body stretch to accommodate his size, his girth.

His big hands around my hips are guiding me. He moves me in rhythm with him until the sound of our lovemaking fills the air. I'm rising up and down on him as I ride him with abandon. I throw my hair back as I uncontrollably shatter in his arms. He pulls me firmly against his groin as he surges against me and finds his own release.

I lean forward, resting my head against his shoulder as our breathing slows.

Sex with Michael feels phenomenal. He's an experienced and exciting lover. He takes my chin and pulls my face to his for a slow, searching kiss.

Then we're finished, and I slowly climb off his lap. I silently pick up our clothes.

Then I take his hand. "Come with me, Michael."

Instead of walking upstairs to the bedroom he shared with his late wife, I pull him with me into my apartment and to my bed.

I feel his warm lips as they kiss my abdomen with reverence. He places his hand over my stomach and says possessively, "Mine."

Then he's kissing me everywhere he can reach.

Michael looks into my eyes as we lay side by side, facing each other. I have one leg thrown over his hip. He takes me slowly, grinding into me in a circular motion. When he hits inside of me like that at different angles, it leaves me breathless and gasping.

He whispers, "Do you like this, Honey? Is it good for you?"

THIRTEEN

"Yes, but Michael, I need... faster, harder... I need more."

"Me too, baby, me too."

He suddenly rolls me under him. He puts his weight on his knees and increases his speed and pressure. Soon, he's pounding into me as he takes me roughly.

My head thrashes against the sheets.

"Michael... Yes! I'm... I'm..."

Michael reaches down between us and thrums my clit.

"Come for me, Honey."

It's an order, and I mindlessly obey. I'm flying as my body clenches helplessly in his arms.

We shout out our completion. He rests my head against his chiseled chest.

I feel him grin into my hair as he states, "If this is what being married will be like, I'm all in."

I give a small laugh at his words, and then he playfully rolls off me and helps me up.

"I believe your shower is big enough for two." Michael picks me up and carries me into my small shower. We wash each other clean in between adoring kisses.

"Damn, I guess we don't have time for anything more. It's almost time to pick the kids up from school."

He gives me one last lingering kiss on my shoulder before he releases me to step out of the shower.

"Let's tell the kids tonight." He says with a smile. "Do you want me to go with you to pick them up?"

"No, why don't you stay here, and then we'll tell them after dinner. If you come with me, they'll be full of questions."

He nods, gives me a quick peck on the lips, and then heads into his home office.

As I pick up the children, I'm quiet, but they chatter away. I glance back at Matthew in the rearview mirror and then over at Megan, wondering how they'll take the news.

Fourteen

Michael

"Can I be in the wedding?" Megan asks immediately after she hears our news.

I smile. "Of course, Megan." I glance at Honey. "We both want you to be in the wedding."

"That'll be so cool!" She replies, her eyes sparkling with excitement.

Matthew's face reflects the complete opposite as he frowns. "Dad? I don't have to be in the wedding, do I?"

"Well, we were kind of hoping you'd carry the rings, Matt," I respond easily.

He continues to frown. "Will I have to dress up?"

"Yes, you'll have to dress up, son. Regardless of whether you're in the wedding or not."

Matthew scrunches his face as if in pain. "I can't drop 'em, right?"

"Right. No dropping of the rings is allowed," I tell him solemnly.

Matthew's face crumbles at my words. "Ah, Dad. Then I don't know... What if I drop 'em?"

"We can talk about it later, Matt. There's nothing to worry about." I say as I place my hand on his shoulder.

Then Matthew turns to Honey. "Will I have to call you mom?"

Honey gives him a soft smile as she shakes her head. "No, Matthew, only if you want to. Michelle was your mother. I'll be your stepmom."

Matthew considers her words. "Stepmom. Lots of kids in my class have stepmoms, but they aren't nearly as nice as you are."

"Thanks. Matt. Why don't you continue to call me, Honey? If you want to call me Mom later, that's okay too," Honey states gently.

FOURTEEN

Matthew gives a solemn nod at Honey's suggestion. I can tell he's thinking things through.

I clear my throat and point out, "Now, we'll all have the same last name. Honey will be my wife, and she'll be Honey Garret. We'll be the Garret family. Won't that be nice?"

Matthew shrugs as he suddenly looks bored. "Yeah, I guess so. Can I go play now?"

I nod. "Sure, you can."

"Okay, cool," Matthew says over his shoulder. He jumps out of his chair and disappears up the stairs, like any other night.

I glance over at Megan, and she's leaning in, talking to Honey.

"So, what color dress will I be wearing? Will I get to hold a bouquet of flowers?" Her eyes sparkle with excitement, her body practically vibrating with anticipation.

"Megan, I'll need your help deciding on colors and all that." Honey smiles over at my daughter. "Let's get together after you come home from school, and you can help me choose everything."

"Everything? Oh my gosh! That's great. It's going to be so much fun! We can pick out our dresses and... Oh, you'd look so good carrying peach roses! Hmm, but I look best in blue, which is a pretty color too..." Megan is practically bursting with fresh ideas.

"Now remember, your father and I decided to keep the wedding small."

"I know, but you still want it to be beautiful! It's so exciting. I've never been in a wedding before!" Megan says, her face glowing.

Honey and I exchange a glance over Megan's head as we share a smile.

Megan finally rushes to her room. "I want to check out different styles of dresses and colors online."

Honey looks up at me and gives me a relieved smile. "They didn't seem to mind."

"Did you think they would?" I frown down at her in disbelief. "Were you worried?"

"I didn't know what to expect. So, maybe?" With a sheepish grin, she admits, "I may have been worried just a little bit."

"Honey, the kids adore you, and so do I. We're going to be one big happy family."

FOURTEEN

Her smile doesn't falter, but her eyes have a wistful look, or is that just my imagination? I reach out and slowly pull Honey into my arms.

"You want this, don't you, Honey? To be married to me?" I ask quietly as I rub my hands up and down her back, trying to chase away any doubts about our future.

She leans her head against my chest for a moment and closes her eyes. I start to frown, but then she lifts her head, and her honey-colored eyes are clear as she meets my gaze.

"Yes, Michael. I want this. I want to be your wife," she says simply.

"Good!" I lean down and give her a quick, hard kiss for her answer.

I let her go reluctantly and walk with her into the kitchen to help with the dishes. Everything is soon put away, and the dishes are stacked in the dishwasher. The only sound is the machine's low hum and the water swishing in the background. Honey turns to me with a warning look on her face.

"Michael, I have a big family." She gives me a searching look. "They will all want to attend the wedding."

I pull her loosely into my arms. "Great. They're your family, so they should be there."

I watch as Honey chews nervously on her lower lip. I can tell something is still bothering her.

"Honey, is something wrong?" I ask gently.

She hesitates, then takes a deep breath as she gives me a tentative smile. "No, not really. I'm sure they'll be fine with the news."

I ask her carefully, "Will your family need a place to stay?"

"No, I'm sure my Aunt Skipper will put them up. They'll want to visit with her anyway. Aunt Skipper's place is huge... we could have the wedding there too."

Honey looks up at me, and her eyes seem brighter. "I need to let my aunt know about the wedding, as well as my cousin Trent and his wife. Paige and my aunt will want to help Megan and me plan everything."

I smile when she makes a point to include my young daughter. That's Honey, always thinking of the children. I reach down and give her another quick kiss.

She arches a brow at me. "As you know, Mr. Garret, seeing the bride before the wedding is bad luck. We should refrain from sleeping together until after we're married."

"Seriously?" I ask in disbelief, hoping she's joking.

Honey laughs softly at the look of disappointment on my face.

"Yes. I'm already wondering what to tell my family," she admits with a grimace. "My dad, and especially my grandpa. They may not be thrilled."

I frown down at her. "I thought we agreed not to mention the baby. Only tell everyone that we're getting married."

"Yes, but... well, my family, they're quick to ask questions and jump to conclusions. So, I don't know. I may have to tell my aunt and Paige." Honey glances up at me and gives me a reassuring smile. "Don't worry. I'll decide when I see them. It will be fine."

I give her another firm hug. "Yes. It will be."

Later, we all gather in the family room, and Honey walks in, holding three bowls of freshly popped popcorn. I smile as she hands one to each of the kids, leaving one for us to share. Megan is sprawled over the armchair, and Matthew is lying on the floor, waiting for the movie to begin.

Honey then sits down beside me on the couch. I reach out, put my arm around Honey's waist, and pull her over closer to me. She gives a contented little smile and snuggles even closer. I look down at her, and while everyone else watches the movie, I watch the flickering light from the TV as it illuminates Honey's lovely face. My eyes rove over her body as I imagine her heavy with my child. I give a contented smile as I find myself liking the idea.

I especially like knowing Honey will be in my bed every single night.

I smell the light fragrance of her honeysuckle shampoo as she leans her head against my shoulder. While everyone, including Honey, seems engrossed in the show, I'm discovering how much I like feeling Honey's lush body pressed against mine. We've never sat this close before while watching TV as a family.

I think of what Honey said about waiting until after we're married to sleep together again. I give a frustrated sigh. Luckily, we've already agreed to get married quickly before the baby starts to show.

I reach out, lightly wrap my arm around Honey, and smile because it feels so right.

FOURTEEN

My lips twist into a grimace as I adjust to a more comfortable position.

I can wait a little longer—I hope!

Fifteen

Honey

That night, after I put on my nightgown and crawl into bed, I smile and rest my head against my pillow. I hug myself as I bask in the thought of being married to Michael!

I suddenly sit straight up in bed as I think again about my family. I know my entire family will want to come to the wedding… my smile slips just a bit.

Then I think of my sisters and brothers. It will be so good to see them again. I've missed all of them. We still stay in touch via email, chat, and the occasional call, but it's just not the same.

There's so much to do before they arrive! My head fills with a list of things I need to complete. My dreams are filled with flowing white dresses and a handsome groom.

The next morning, I ring my cousin Trent's wife, Paige.

"Hey, would you be free for lunch?" I ask in a hopeful tone.

"Sure," Paige answers. "I'd love to meet up, Honey."

We decide on a time and place. Shot in the Dark, a local pub at one o'clock. I call my Aunt Skipper and invite her as well.

I arrive before Paige and my aunt and grab a booth—the hum of the conversation and the clinking of glasses a familiar backdrop of sound.

I glance up to see my aunt and Paige walk in together. I wave them over. My Aunt Skipper is an attractive older woman. She was a beauty in her heyday, as she puts it. She still is. Her gray hair is always perfectly styled, and she loves to shop. Her favorite store is called Patchingtons. I wouldn't put it past her to be the main reason they stay in business.

I watch as Paige makes her way over to the booth. That girl gets attention wherever she goes. She's a stunning blonde with an extremely curvy figure. She takes all the male attention in stride nowadays, so it's hard to believe it used to bother her.

She showed me pictures of before she met my cousin, Trent. She wore big oversized sweaters and considered herself a geek. I giggle as that part hasn't changed. However, I prefer to call her a whiz instead of a geek when it comes to computers.

I stand up and give them a hug. "Hey, ladies. I'm glad you could meet me for lunch."

My aunt returns my hug.

"Of course, sugar." She states in her Southern draw, "My, you look happy. You're practically glowing."

I smile at the compliment. "Thanks, Aunt Skipper."

We all sit down and place our order when the server comes by. We come here quite often for lunch, so we barely glance at the menu.

Paige turns to me and states, "Okay, , Spill! It sounds like you have news."

I look at Paige and then my aunt. "Michael asked me to marry him."

"What? That's wonderful," Paige says with a delighted grin. "Congratulations! I know you've had a thing for your boss ever since you started working there."

FIFTEEN

My aunt responds more slowly, "I'm glad to hear he's finally come around and noticed what was right beneath his nose this whole time." She gives a slight frown. "I don't see a flashy diamond on your ring finger."

I feel the heat as it covers my cheeks in a dull red. Darn. I completely forgot about an engagement ring. Maybe I should have waited...

"We wanted to take our time picking one out. Everything happened so fast. We just told the children last night."

"When's the wedding?" My aunt asks at the same time that Paige leans forward. "Have you picked a date?"

"Not really. That's one of the reasons I wanted to talk to you both." My eyes dart to my aunt. "Skipper, I was hoping we could have the ceremony at your house."

She gives me a delighted smile. "Of course you can, . Just let me know when."

"Well, I haven't told my dad and the family yet, but I'm sure they'll all want to attend."

My aunt nods. "They can stay at my house. I've got plenty of room. In fact, the last time we all got together was when Trent and Paige tied the knot."

"Thanks, Aunt Skipper. We were thinking of having the wedding maybe at the end of next month. Would that be, okay?" I chew on my bottom lip.

"That soon?" My aunt asks as her eyes widen in surprise. I can see the wheels turning in her mind as she takes another sip of her iced tea.

"Hmmm... I have a glowing bride wanting a fast wedding. Anything else you have to tell us, sugar?" My Aunt Skipper raises her eyebrow in my direction.

I feel my flush deepen even further to a guilty red as she studies my reaction to her question.

Paige gasps. "Skipper! I can't believe you're asking Honey a question like that! I'm sure it's not what you think, why--"

I reach out with my hand and cover Paige's as I interrupt, "She's right. I'm pregnant." I give a sheepish shrug.

Paige blinks and gives me a startled look. "Oh. Is everyone happy about this?" She asks tentatively.

"By everyone, if you mean Michael, then yes. He likes being a father," I state quietly.

My aunt gives me a shrewd look. "That's good. While every man likes fathering a baby, not all of them like the consequences that come after," my aunt says dryly.

Then, her gaze turns compassionate. "Does he love you, Honey?"

I choose my words carefully. "He cares about me, but love? No, I don't think he's in love with me," I admit with a bit of longing.

"But you're in love with him," my aunt states with a knowing look.

I nod, even though it wasn't a question.

My aunt asks softly, "Will that be enough?"

Paige listens silently to our exchange.

I give a slightly sad smile.

"I asked myself the same question..." I look directly at my aunt and say firmly, "Yes, I'll make it enough." As she reaches out to squeeze my hand, the words earnestly pour out of me, "We get along so well, and I love his children as if they were my own. I can't imagine my life without all of them in it."

I suddenly stop to catch my breath. Then, at a slower pace, I say, "I know Michael will be a faithful, caring husband." I glance over at my aunt and Paige. "I could raise this baby by myself. But I want—I choose to raise this child in a loving home. Even if Michael never returns my feelings. I know he'll love this baby. He's a good man, and he's a great father."

"Humph." Paige and I both look at Skipper as she continues, "Well, I, for one, have seen how he looks at you, and it isn't fatherly... at all. You know I disagree with people getting married just because they got knocked up... but in your case? I think it will only be a matter of time before that man wises up to the truth."

The server sets down our meals. Before we take a bite, my aunt and Paige both raise their glasses, and I raise my water glass for their toast.

"Congratulations on the baby and your upcoming nuptials, Honey," Paige says with a smile.

"Thank you. By the way, we're not mentioning the baby to anyone. Even the children don't know yet. Okay?"

They both nod their heads, then my Aunt Skipper says, "Girls, we have a wedding to plan!"

FIFTEEN

A few days later, Megan sees me waiting for her after school. She rushes over, her face alight with excitement, and scrambles into the front seat.

"I thought there was something wrong with the clock," she says, buckling up. "The entire day just seemed to drag by."

I smile. "Megan, it felt the same way for me, too."

"Is your aunt and Paige meeting us there?"

"Yes, they're probably waiting for us now," I reply as I pull into the Jacksonville traffic. "Your dad picked up Matthew, and they're spending the afternoon together," I explain as I turn into a parking space in front of the bridal shop.

Megan is practically buzzing with anticipation as we approach the store. Once inside, her eyes widen in awe as she surveys the vast array of dresses.

"Holy smokes! Look at all these dresses!" she exclaims.

We hear my Aunt Skipper's voice, "There they are. Honey, Megan over here, girls."

I lean down and suggest, "Megan, I thought you and Paige could pick out your dresses first, and then I'll look at the wedding dresses."

"Really?" Her eyes shimmer with excitement.

"Yes." I give her a playful wink. "You have to pick out the color and style of your dress. I already know mine will be white and long."

Megan giggles and rushes over to the bridesmaids' dresses that line an entire wall.

Soon, everyone's arms are filled with possible choices. The saleslady wheels over a rack, and we hang up our selections.

I go into a dressing room with Megan, and Aunt Skipper goes in with Paige. After an hour of trying on gowns, I slip a silky cornflower blue dress over Megan's head and zip it up. When Megan turns around, I give a delighted smile.

"I think this is the one," I say knowingly as Megan looks in the mirror.

I watch as her eyes light up. "I do, too. It's gorgeous!" She gives a little jump of joy. "I love it!"

"You look beautiful in that dress, Megan, and you'll be able to wear it again, maybe to a party, a dance, or a charity event."

She nods, but her eyes never leave her reflection as she turns this way and that in front of the three-way mirror.

"Let's show it to Paige and Aunt Skip," I suggest with a smile.

Megan leaves the dressing room and proudly shows off her beautiful dress.

My Aunt Skipper smiles as she states, "Megan, you're just about the prettiest thing I've seen today."

I watch Megan give a swirl, the full skirt of the dress billowing out.

"Blue is definitely your color," I tell her with a fond smile.

Next, Paige walks out of the dressing room, wearing a frothy blue-green dress that complements her unusual eyes. While not matching, the two dresses coordinate perfectly with their similar hues of blue and green.

Megan looks at me and says, "Okay, now it's your turn, Honey."

The saleslady carefully hands me the first dress. We all step into their group dressing room, and I try it on.

While it's lovely, it's not the dress for me. I try on about three more. Then the saleslady knocks on the door.

"I wanted to show you a dress that we just got in. It matches what you said you were looking for." She holds up the classic gown. "I thought you might like it."

I smile as I reach out to take the dress. The fabric is made of the finest silk and seems to glow softly in the light.

"Oh, it's beautiful," I state in awe.

It has a sweetheart neckline, no lace, no frills. As Paige slips it over my head, I hear the whisper of silk as it settles over my frame. The dress is a simple yet elegant sheath, its clean lines and flowing silhouette accentuating my figure. The silk fabric feels smooth against my skin, and the sweetheart neckline draws attention to the creamy white skin of my neck and collarbones.

My aunt states softly, "Oh Lordy, but you look fine in that dress, Honey."

I smooth my hands down the sides. I love the silky feel of it. I glance in the mirror again, admiring the graceful simplicity of the gown.

Paige says excitedly, "Turn around. Let's see it from every angle."

Megan chimes in, "It makes your waist look so tiny. I love the neckline."

"Well, Honey?" Paige asks, "What do you think of the dress?"

I smile at my reflection and then turn to the women.

"I love it." I smile. "This is the one for me."

My aunt states in a sincere voice, "You'll be a lovely bride."

Sixteen

Michael

I glance over at my son as he slams the car door shut. "How was school today?"

Matthew shrugs and states, "Fine. I had fun in gym class. We ran laps."

"I remember when I thought running laps was fun," I tell him with a chuckle as I pull onto the road.

As I slow the car, Matthew looks out the windows. "I thought we were going to the men's shop?"

"We are. Later," I say with a grin as I parallel park in front of well-known jewelers. "Right now, I need your help picking out a ring for Honey,"

As we enter the jewelry store, a wave of cool air washes over us. A saleslady glances up. "What can I help you with today?" She asks with a polite smile.

"I'm here to pick out an engagement ring," I respond with a wide grin.

The saleslady's smile brightens as she waves us over to the counter. Matthew's eyes shine with astonishment as he spies the dazzling display of diamond rings.

"Well, what do you think, son? Which ring would Honey like?"

Matthew suddenly gets a thoughtful look on his face as he carefully examines the selection. "I'm not sure," he says with a shrug.

I look up at the saleslady, who suggests, "Why don't I show you our most popular wedding sets?"

I nod, and she directs my attention to a few different styles, but nothing she shows me feels right for Honey.

Matthew, who has wandered over to another counter, turns, his eyes sparkling with excitement, and states, "Dad! I found it!" He waves me over and points down at a beautiful topaz ring, the exact color of warm honey. "See? Isn't it pretty? The color reminds me of Honey!" He looks up at me with eager eyes. "I know she'll like this one. It's perfect!"

I put my hand on Matthew's shoulder as I bend closer to examine the ring. I glance up as the saleslady approaches. Her smile falters slightly as she shakes her head. "These are gemstones. Most women prefer a diamond solitaire—"

Matthew looks crestfallen at the woman's words, but I interrupt her with, "May we see this ring, please?"

Her smile thins, but she takes out the topaz ring and lays it before us. She makes a final attempt to dissuade me as she states firmly, "This is an emerald cut topaz. Though I agree this ring is quite attractive, topaz is a common gemstone..."

Her voice trails off as I announce, "We'll take this one. Can you size it for us?"

"Yes, of course." As I tell the saleslady the size, I glance down at my son, whose eyes are still shining with excitement and pride. I look again at the display. I point to something that catches my eye and glance questioningly at the sales lady.

"Would you have something like this that would work with the ring we picked out?" I ask an idea forming in my mind.

The saleslady's smile brightens significantly.

"Yes, sir. Let me see what we have."

As she goes to consult with the jeweler, I squeeze Matthew's shoulder.

"You're right, son. That is the perfect ring for Honey." I smile as I imagine how it will look on her slender finger.

We're instructed to return for the rings in a couple of hours. Matthew and I spend the time being fitted for our tuxedos for the wedding. The Taylor only needs to know the color of our cummerbunds and bow ties; otherwise, we're done.

Soon, we're headed back to the jewelers. This time, I have the saleslady's complete approval as she shows us the finished product.

I glance over at Matthew. "Well, what do you think?"

He's practically bouncing up and down with his excitement. "Honey is going to love it!"

When we enter the house, Matthew throws his backpack on the bench in the foyer, and before he disappears up the stairs,

I remind him, "We've already made plans to go out to dinner tonight. We'll leave as soon as Honey and Megan get home."

We both turn as we hear car doors slamming.

"That sounds like the girls now," I say.

Megan and Honey enter the house with huge smiles on their faces.

I ask with a grin, "I take it the shopping was successful?"

They both nod their heads as Megan states with a happy smile, "My dress is a beautiful blue! And you should see the wedding dress..." her voice trails away as she glances over at Honey.

Then she looks up at me and explains, "I was told not to tell anyone about the bridal dress as it's supposed to be a surprise." Her eyes solemn.

I give her a serious nod back as I say, "I totally understand. But I know you'll look very pretty in blue."

As my eyes meet Honey's, we share a smile. I rub my hands together. "Everybody ready?"

Once we arrive at the restaurant, I step around to open the door for Honey and the children to enter. The warm, inviting scent of freshly baked bread and simmering sauces wafts

SIXTEEN

through the air, filling our senses with anticipation. The upscale restaurant is adorned with elegant décor, soft lighting, and a peaceful ambiance that creates a sense of sophistication and refinement.

As we are shown to our table, we can't help but marvel at the breathtaking view of the St. John's River that stretches out before us. I notice the children lower their voices to a hushed murmur as they lean forward for a better look.

Honey glances over at me with a soft smile. "This is nice. I guess I wasn't expecting anything so grand."

I shrug as I reply, "I didn't want you to have to cook tonight, after going shopping."

There's a lull of silence as we all look over the menu. After we've given the server our order, I raise my water glass.

"To a beautiful wedding."

My entire family smiles as we carefully clink our glasses together and drink to my toast.

Megan is the first to break the relative silence. Her eyes gleam with excitement as she tells us about the rows and rows of beautiful dresses. She describes her dress and Paige's in greater detail.

When it's Matthew's turn, I give him a warning look, but he just grins back and proceeds to talk about the tuxedo fitting. I try not to laugh at his pained expression. His description of our time at the men's shop sounds a lot more tortuous than I remember it being.

When the server brings our dinner, the conversation is muted for a few minutes as we savor the fine food.

I look over at Honey. "Isn't this nice? You didn't have to prepare anything, and there's no cleanup." I give her a playful wink.

Honey leans back in her chair, a contented smile playing on her lips.

"I have to admit that I'm feeling quite pampered," she says, her voice soft and relaxed.

After a delicious dinner, the server clears our plates and presents us with a dessert menu. Honey and I exchange a knowing glance. We've already decided on our desserts: cheesecake for her and apple pie ala mode for me. The children both order chocolate cake.

As we wait for our desserts to arrive, I reach into my pocket and pull out a small velvet box. I stand up and kneel before Honey. I can feel my heart pounding in my chest.

"Honey," I begin, my voice low. "I've already asked you to marry me. This will make it official."

Honey's eyes widen in surprise, and she starts to smile. I open the velvet box for her to see the ring.

I hear her gasp, "Michael! It's beautiful," she whispers in awe.

I stand and slip the ring onto her finger. I smile down at her as I see how the ring looks on her.

"It suits you," I tell her, my voice husky.

She smiles up at me and says, "It's perfect."

I stand there, lost in the contented gleam radiating from Honey's eyes. I blink and clear my throat.

"Matthew helped pick it out," I murmur when I can finally speak.

The spell is broken as we both turn toward Matthew, his face beams with pride.

"It's topaz. The color reminded me of you," he states in a delighted voice. Then he admits, "Dad added the starbursts of diamonds around it."

My eyes dart to Honey's as she glances down at the ring, the overhead lights reflecting off the glittering jewels.

"I love it," she says simply, her eyes filled with joy.

I return her smile and feel a sudden and unexpected tightness in my chest due to the look on her upturned face.

Seventeen

Honey

Michael walks into the kitchen, his presence immediately warming the space. He leans in close and presses a slow, lingering kiss to my lips.

"Good morning, Honey," he murmurs in that low, rich voice of his. Then, in a whisper meant only for me, he adds, "I can't wait for us to finally share a marriage bed."

I can feel the heat rise in my cheeks, spreading across my face. I glance around, making sure the kids aren't nearby, and Michael laughs softly, his eyes gleaming with mischief.

"They're upstairs, still getting ready for school," he assures me with a grin.

"In that case..." I tug him down again, capturing his lips in another kiss, more intense this time. We only break apart when we hear the clatter of footsteps on the stairs.

As Megan and Matthew rush into the kitchen for their cereal, I share a quick glance with Michael.

"My family's arriving today," I remind him. "I'll be meeting them over at Aunt Skipper's, and I'll have the kids with me after I pick them up from school."

I add, "They've heard all about the Garret family and seen photos, but now they're eager to meet all of you in person."

Michael winks. "I'm looking forward to it," he replies, his grin widening. "It should be fun."

"Dinner is at Aunt Skip's tonight, around six."

He nods. "Six o'clock it is. Don't worry, I'll be there."

SEVENTEEN

Later, I pull into Aunt Skipper's driveway, glancing up at her grand estate. Her house always gives me a sense of nostalgia—so large and Southern, like something out of a storybook. Skipper is proud of her Southern roots, but she carries it with that effortless charm, never taking herself too seriously.

The front door swings open before I even knock, and Aunt Skipper's arms envelop me in a warm hug.

"Honey, I thought for sure it was your family pulling up," she teases, her eyes flicking to the driveway. "They should be arriving any minute."

I follow her into the spacious kitchen, where the smell of fresh-baked biscuits hangs in the air. As she turns back to me, I hold up my hand, flashing my engagement ring. Her smile grows even wider as she admires the topaz surrounded by diamonds.

"Matthew helped his father pick it out," I explain.

"It's stunning, Honey. The color is just so you," she remarks, her voice full of affection.

"I told Matthew the same thing. I absolutely love it."

Aunt Skipper gives me a knowing look. "How's everything with the baby?"

I beam. "Michael's coming with me to the next doctor's appointment. It's scheduled for right after we get back from the honeymoon."

Her approving nod follows. "And who's looking after the kids while you two are gone?"

"Michael's cousin. They've got kids around the same age. They'll be at the wedding, and then Megan and Matthew will head home with them afterward."

"Sounds like you've got it all planned out," she says with a smile.

"Thanks for letting us have the wedding here," I tell her sincerely, appreciating how much it means.

She waves a hand. "This house is far too big for just me rattling around. I love hosting weddings—it reminds me of my own marriage to Martin." Her eyes turn misty for a moment before refocusing on me. "The caterer and florist have everything under control. It'll be perfect."

Just then, the doorbell rings, and we both hurry to the foyer. Aunt Skipper throws open the door with a flourish.

"Here they are!"

SEVENTEEN

The room fills with warmth and laughter as my three brothers, two sisters, and my father bustle in, their voices filling the air. Last, moving more slowly, comes my grandfather, with his caregiver, Lock, close behind.

Grandfather walks with a cane now; he feels it's more stately than a walker. His hair, once red like my father's, is now snowy white, and his eyes are the same sharp green as ever. He looks like an older version of Dad, who's already graying at the temples.

I carefully hug Grandpa, who studies me with that same all-seeing gaze, before I turn to Lock. His strong arms give me a gruff but warm hug. Lock hasn't changed at all—He's built like a bodybuilder. Stocky and tall. As usual, he doesn't have much to say. He's still the quiet, strong presence he's always been.

"I'm so glad you're here, Grandpa. Lock, thank you for coming," I say warmly before turning to the rest of my family.

We all head into the kitchen, where Aunt Skipper's sweet tea is ready for everyone. The house feels a little smaller with my large family filling it, their voices bouncing off the high ceilings. Once the greetings settle, we head outside to gather their luggage. My two younger sisters, Savannah and Georgia Ann, chatter excitedly as we haul the bags upstairs.

Savannah, at seventeen, is already graceful and confident, while Georgia Ann, at twelve, is full of wide-eyed energy. Both have inherited the reddish hair from my father.

"We're finally here!" Georgia Ann says with a grin, throwing herself onto one of the beds prompts her head on her hand. "Honey, you look so happy! I bet you can't wait for the wedding!"

I smile at her excitement. "Do you mind not being in the wedding party?"

Georgia Ann pulls a face. "At first, I was a little disappointed, but Savannah pointed out that if you asked us to be in the wedding, you'd have to ask the boys, and—"

Savannah cuts her off by throwing a pillow, which hits Georgia Ann square in the face. My oldest sister finishes the sentence by dryly stating, "And then there'd be more of us in the wedding than there are guests."

Georgia Ann, used to being the baby, just laughs and tucks the pillow under her arm.

Savannah turns to me, wide-eyed with curiosity. "So... when do we get to meet your fiancé?"

I chuckle at the dreamy look in Savannah's eyes. "I think it's so romantic that you fell in love with your boss," she gushes.

"You'll meet him at dinner," I remind her with a smile. "And you'll meet the children after I pick them up from school."

Georgia Ann blinks up at me, rolling onto her back as she hugs the pillow to her chest. "Megan's ten years old, right?"

I nod. "Yes, and you'll like her—and Matthew too. He turns seven in a few months."

I sit down on the bed beside Georgia Ann, facing Savannah, who's perched on the other bed.

"They're wonderful kids," I say with a warm smile, hoping to ease any nerves they might have about meeting them.

Savannah gives me a sly look. "You've always said that in your letters. But I want to hear more about Michael," she teases.

Georgia Ann leans forward, casting me an apologetic glance. "Savannah's always been suspicious about what you didn't say about their father." She shoots Savannah an exaggerated eye roll. "She's constantly talking about boys."

Savannah rolls her eyes right back. "Georgia Ann is still a child, so she doesn't talk about boys—yet," she says in a superior voice.

I laugh, shaking my head. "I'm glad to see your bickering hasn't changed." Then, softening, I add, "I've missed you two."

Savannah grins. "Aww, we've missed you too, Honey."

Just then, a loud knock comes at the door. We all look up as it swings open, revealing my oldest brother, Brighton. He takes after my mother with his light hair and brown eyes.

"Hey, you girls can't keep Honey all to yourselves," he says, half-joking.

Savannah and Georgia Ann start to protest, but Brighton and I exchange knowing looks, ignoring their groaning complaints. I stand and pull Georgia Ann off the bed.

"Brighton's right," I say with a grin. "Let's go downstairs so we can all catch up together."

As we head down the wide staircase, we're joined by the twins, David and Daniel. Though not identical, they're as close as brothers can be. David, with his dark hair and brown eyes, is the tech-savvy one, while Daniel, with his blonde hair and green eyes, is always outdoors. Their differences only make their bond stronger.

I fall into step beside Brighton, glancing at him curiously. "So, how are things back home?"

"Same old, same old," he replies with a shrug. Then he pauses, his lips curling into a grin. "But I do have some news."

I raise my eyebrows. "You got the job, didn't you?"

His grin widens, a flash of white teeth showing. "Yeah, I did."

"Brighton! That's amazing!" I exclaim, hugging him even though we're still navigating the stairs. "I'm so happy for you—congratulations!"

He beams with pride, the weight of accomplishment visible in his eyes. "Thanks, sis," he says, clearly pleased.

We reach the kitchen, refilling our drinks before heading out to the covered terrace where Dad and Aunt Skipper are already seated, deep in conversation. As we step outside, they both glance up, smiling and we all take a seat around them.

"Where's Grandpa?" I ask when I don't see him among the others.

Dad looks over at me, his expression gentle. "Lock said he's resting," he explains, adding with reassurance, "They'll join us soon enough."

I nod, though a flicker of concern lingers. "I noticed Grandpa seemed a little more frail than usual."

Dad sighs, nodding solemnly. "Yes, he's been relying on Lock a lot more these days."

Aunt Skipper clears her throat, her voice taking on that no-nonsense tone we all know. "Let's take turns catching up. Ezra, why don't you start?" she suggests, looking at Dad with a raised eyebrow.

Eighteen

Michael

I push the open file away from me on my desk, blinking my tired eyes. Hours of poring over every detail have left them blurry. My shoulders ache from the strain, and I hunch forward to relieve the tension. As I glance around my office, the city skyline stretches out before me.

The office itself is a reflection of my professional dedication to the law: Traditional heavy wooden furniture polished to a high shine. Floor-to-ceiling windows dominate one wall, offering panoramic views of the city. A wide desk sits in the center, its surface cluttered with legal documents and a half-empty coffee mug. Bookshelves line one side of the room, filled with law tomes and a few personal favorites.

I lean back in my chair, allowing my thoughts to wander to my upcoming wedding. The stress of the case fades into the background as I think about the changes being married will have on my life.

My kids are excited. Well, Megan is excited. Matthew really doesn't care. He's such a typical boy. He seemed happy that Honey would be an official part of our family, and he was pleased knowing we would all have the same last name. He seems to like the idea of Honey as his stepmother and my wife.

My wife... I haven't really stopped to think beyond what needed to be done. I'm the one who got Honey pregnant. The logical thing is for us to marry. My kids love her, and I care about her. It's the right thing to do. For them, for Honey, and for me.

These past two years, Honey has been more than just a great nanny to my children. She was there when they needed her. Yet, It's more than that, more than decorating their rooms with balloons and fixing their favorite foods—she makes them feel special. She makes them feel loved.

Honey was supposed to be off-limits. But it's way too late to close that barn door. She's already carrying my child. Being married to Honey shouldn't be that much different than our current relationship with each other…Right?

My frown slowly turns into a masculine grin. There will be one big difference. Sex. I will be sharing a bed with Honey.

And let's face it, making love to Honey is pretty damn great. We're as compatible in bed as we are out of it. My smile broadens as I imagine what it will be like to be able to make love to Honey every single night if I want.

As for the baby, I've always liked being a dad. Oh sure, I was worried at first. I mean, having a child changes your life completely. Suddenly, you're responsible for this little person. You worry about how you're going to provide for them. And not just financially. Oh no, you worry if you're raising them right or being too strict or too lenient.

I remember when we found out Michelle was pregnant. I was so damn scared. She was bursting with excitement, so I tried to hide my uncertainty. Then, I held Megan for the first time. I'll never forget how that tiny little girl melted my heart. One look at her, and that was it. I loved her so instantly, so completely, that it shook me to the core.

Later, when Matthew came along, I didn't know if I could love another child as much as I loved our first. Yet, the same thing happened when I held my son. I fell in love with him right then. I know I'll feel the same way about this child. Yes, children change your life... for the better.

I wearily glance back down at the file on my desk. I've been busy catching up on the new case—the one I never wanted. The one I did my damnedest to turn down. I've had to farm out some of my other cases just to make time for this one.

I tried very hard to reject Colleen's offer. Not that it did any good, I think, with a scowl. She and her clients made it very plain they wouldn't take no for an answer.

On top of their thinly veiled threats, I continue to receive warnings from Colleen and the mob. I guess I shouldn't call them that, but it's the truth.

I can feel the urgency of getting Victor exonerated. I just hope I can make that happen. The more I look over his case, the worse it looks for him. I called in my team, and we've made quite a bit of headway in gathering information, but so far, we have found nothing that will help get a non-guilty verdict.

EIGHTEEN

I feel like time is running out. I grimace. The only thing worse than representing the son of an infamous mobster is taking over their criminal defense at the last minute!

I glance up as my admin comes to the door, "Michael, there are two men here to talk to you about the Victor Mazarano case."

I nod. "That's fine, Nancy. Please show them in."

Two men grimly enter my office in their immaculate suits and take a seat. The tension in the air suddenly feels heavy, like a thick fog.

"Gentlemen, what can I do for you?" I ask curiously once they've settled in their chairs.

"We're here for an update, Garret," the smaller of the two men states. They both have black oily hair slicked back off their foreheads. The smaller of the men, Marcel, has beady little eyes and a pockmarked face. He reminds me of a rat in how his eyes dart around the room, and he looks over his shoulder constantly. Meanwhile, the stockier man, Bruno, appears to be the muscle man of the bunch. He doesn't say much; he just sits there looking intimidating.

"I don't really have anything to report," I tell them flatly. "My team and I are still going through all of the paperwork."

They don't immediately answer. Instead, they look at each other, and then their gazes narrow on me.

"Garret, I'm sure we don't need to remind you that Vito Mazarano has asked for an update every week. And Vito's not a patient man," Marcel says, his voice dripping with menace.

I swallow hard, trying to steel myself against their intimidation. "I am aware. However, my team and I are still reviewing all of the depositions and details of his son's case."

Bruno leans forward, his eyes boring into mine. "You need to find out who killed Zappo."

I nod and mutter, "I understand." I lean forward. "But In order to make that happen, I need to speak with the accused, Victor Mazarano."

The two men glance at each other uneasily at my words.

"He was granted bail with an electronic bracelet. I know his father is keeping him hidden and secure, but I need answers," I state bluntly.

I lean back in my chair and steeple my fingers. "If I am to represent my client effectively, I need to know what happened that night. Period." My gaze doesn't waiver.

Marcel finally gives me a curt nod. "I'll see what I can do."

I state grimly, "Good. Thank you."

As they stand to leave, Marcel looks down at me.

"A weekly progress report, Garret. No excuses."

I can hear the hidden threat in his voice and grimly nod my head in agreement.

As they exit my office, I can't help but feel a wave of dread wash over me. I know I'm in over my head asking to speak directly with the son of a known leader of the mob.

I have always tried to keep my family life well away from my professional life. Being a criminal attorney means that I often deal with unsavory characters.

I don't like to mix what I do with how I live. The lines have been blurring lately, and I don't like it.

I have always believed that everyone is entitled to fair representation and that they are innocent until proven guilty. But again, that doesn't mean I want to take most of my clients home for dinner. I think grimly. My job should be just that—my job.

I will do whatever I have to do to keep my family safe.

I glance up at the clock, and it's almost five. Nancy, my admin, left about thirty minutes ago. I better leave now if I don't want to be late for dinner with Honey's family. As I gather my papers and stuff them into my briefcase, my office door is thrown open.

I glance up to see Colleen. She gives me a sly smile.

"Vito Mazarano has made arrangements for you to meet his son tonight."

I give her a sharp look. "When? I'm meeting my fiancée's family at six o'clock."

Colleen narrows her eyes and leans against my desk.

"If Vito Mazarano arranges a meeting." She glances at me in warning. "It's in your best interest to attend."

"Dammit, Colleen. This is my first time meeting Honey's family. They just arrived today from out of town."

As she just continues to look at me unblinkingly, I mutter, "I'm getting married this weekend. I've already told this to you and your client—"

"Michael, this may be your only chance to meet the defendant." She glances down at her nails indifferently. "You can come with me now, or I can let Vito Mazarano know that the reason you couldn't make it is that you were running late for a dinner date." She glances at me, and her dark eyes show no emotion.

"The choice is yours," Colleen states coldly.

Nineteen

Honey

I stare blankly down at my phone, my heart sinking. Aunt Skipper notices the change in my expression.

"Honey? Is everything alright?" she asks, her voice filled with concern.

I glance up, forcing a smile. "Yes, everything's fine. It's just... um... Michael won't be able to make it tonight."

A hush falls over the room as my words hang in the air. I feel the weight of everyone's eyes on me, each one filled with a mix of disappointment and confusion.

NINETEEN

My father frowns, his disbelief evident. "Did I hear you right? Your fiancé won't be meeting us tonight?"

I swallow hard, my mouth suddenly dry. "Yes, that's what his text says," I mumble.

I raise my head and turn to my aunt, pleading with my eyes. She immediately smiles, a reassuring gesture.

"I'm sure it was extremely important, or he'd be here," Aunt Skipper states firmly.

She turns to my father and grandfather. "You'll have to wait to meet Michael another time. But that just means more fried shrimp for the rest of us!" she says cheerily, trying to lighten the mood.

I give my aunt a grateful look as everyone laughs, and we hear a few people comment about her famous fried shrimp.

Just as the doorbell chimes, my cousin Trent and his wife, Paige, arrive. They're immediately enveloped in hugs. Trent, a tall blonde built like a football player, and Paige make a striking pair with their blonde good looks.

I go to check on the children who are playing outside with my youngest sister, Georgia Ann.

"Megan, Matthew, I wanted to let you know that your father won't be able to make it to dinner tonight," I inform them. "Something came up at the office."

Megan's face falls. "Wow. I'm sorry, Honey. I know you wanted to introduce him to your family."

Matthew shrugs and continues to throw a ball to my sister.

"I'll let you know when it's time to wash up for dinner," I say over my shoulder as I walk back onto the covered terrace.

As I enter from outside, I hear my father say sharply, "Missing his first meal with us? That doesn't say much for his character."

I give a relieved smile as I hear my cousin Trent's voice.

"Michael Garret is a good man. He's also a very reputable attorney," he states in Michael's defense. "He's currently working on a high-profile murder case. Victor Mazarano. If Michael said something came up, you can be assured it was something he couldn't get out of."

As I walk into the room, my grandfather looks over at Trent.

"What was the man's name again? The fellow accused of murder?" My grandfather asks quietly.

NINETEEN

Trent glances around the room. "Victor Mazarano," he repeats grimly. "His father is Vito Mazarano—"

The twins burst into the room; their faces flushed with excitement. "Aunt Skipper said everybody needs to wash up for dinner!"

Paige and I head to the kitchen.

"What can we do to help, Skipper?" Paige asks my aunt.

"I'm just about ready to start frying the shrimp," Aunt Skipper admits with a smile. "I figure it will be a good half hour before everyone's washed up and sitting around the table."

Paige and I laugh as we look around the kitchen in surprise.

"Aunt Skip, it looks like everything is already prepared," I say, turning to my aunt with amazement. "Did you hire a caterer?"

My aunt looks up proudly. "Yes. You were right, Honey. It made everything so much easier. But I didn't trust anyone else with the shrimp or biscuits. They have to be cooked at the last minute and served piping hot."

"You won't get an argument out of us," Paige says with a smile. "Honey and I will be in charge of getting the food to the tables while you finish the shrimp."

My aunt gives us both a fond smile. Expertly dipping a shrimp in the batter, she pops it in the hot oil. The tantalizing aroma of frying cornbread batter fills the air.

I lean toward Paige. "Let me call in the boys to help us."

I gather my brothers, and we have all the hot food transferred to the dining room in no time.

"Don't take off the lids until Aunt Skip brings in the shrimp and biscuits."

They nod, and I don't even reprimand them when they sneak peeks into a few of the containers. I'm curious myself about the contents.

When my aunt comes in with two huge bowls of golden-brown shrimp and a basket of melt-in-your-mouth homemade biscuits, we peel back the lids to reveal perfectly grilled vegetables, baked potatoes with all the fixings, and a German chocolate cake for dessert.

"You didn't make coconut cake?" Brighton says in surprise.

"Not tonight," my aunt says. "Don't worry, you'll get a slice before you leave for home, boy."

The smell of shrimp has everyone scurrying into the dining room.

My father comes in and tells me, "I told the kids that dinner was ready. They're washing their hands."

"Thanks, Dad," I say with a sincere smile.

Soon, we're all filling our dishes and finding a place at the crowded dining room table. The conversation is lively as we talk about what's been happening in my hometown and the upcoming wedding this weekend. The laughter and chatter fill the air as we catch up on each other's lives.

I feel a touch nostalgic as I glance around the room. It's a reminder of how much I appreciate these moments together, catching up and appreciating each other's company.

I glance at Megan and Matthew; they seem to be enjoying my loud, boisterous family.

I stand and walk over to the sideboard, where the large sheet cake sits untouched, taking center stage. I cut into it with a flourish and dish out generous servings onto the smaller plates.

Turning to the room, I announce, "Who wants a slice of German chocolate cake?"

As the evening draws to an end, my Aunt Skipper asks, "Honey, do you want to prepare a plate for Michael?"

"No, thanks." I turn toward my aunt. "I was hoping he'd still be able to stop by, but..." my voice trails off as she pats my arm.

"I'm sure it was something he had no control over, Honey," she says softly.

Disappointment sweeps through me, and a sigh escapes my lips. "I know, but Dad and Grandpa—"

My aunt interrupts with, "They understand that when it comes to business, we can't always drop everything."

I nod as I murmur, "Thanks, Aunt Skip. I just really wanted everyone to meet..."

"And you wanted Michael to make a good impression." My aunt grins. "I still remember what it's like to introduce the man you love to your family." My aunt smiles with a faraway look in her eyes.

"My father didn't know what to make of Martin the first time they met." She suddenly quirks an eyebrow at me. "On second thought, maybe it's best that Michael couldn't make it tonight."

She wraps an arm around me and gives me a reassuring hug.

Then states firmly, "Fortunately, they'll have plenty of time to meet before the wedding this weekend."

The moon cast a silvery light on us as I finally bundle the children into the car and head home. I glance in the review mirror and see that both children are nodding off in their seats. I smile at the evidence that they had fun today.

It was good to spend time with my family. At times, they made me laugh out loud, and at other times, like with my brother Brighton, I got to share in his success.

My brows furrow as I think about my father and grandfather. They were expecting to meet Michael and get to know him. After all, he's marrying their oldest child and grandchild. While they both can appear stern, I know they care for me.

I feel like I disappointed them tonight...I make a face. No, Michael disappointed them... Actually, if I'm honest, Michael disappointed me. He knew how important this was.

I try to shake off my emotions because I know that Michael intended to be there tonight. So, it makes me wonder what might have happened.

When I pull up to the darkened house, I know that Michael isn't home yet. Will this be another night when he doesn't come home until morning?

I wearily help the children out of the car. They rouse just enough to stumble into the house and drag themselves to their bedrooms. I follow behind them, then tuck them in. Megan is too exhausted to protest as I tuck the covers around her. When I reach Matthew, he's already dead to the world. I lean down and give him a gentle goodnight kiss before I tiptoe out of his room.

I slowly make my way downstairs. I'm almost as exhausted as the children. I grimace. I didn't know being pregnant could make you feel so tired. My limbs feel heavy as I decide to relax for a minute on the sofa. I rest my head back, hug a throw pillow to my chest, and fall instantly into a deep sleep.

When my eyes flutter open, I'm being scooped up by strong arms and carried to my apartment. The dim light of early morning bathes the rooms in a soft light. I look up to see Michael as he tenderly sets me on my bed.

I reach out and run my fingers lightly down his face. His cheeks feel rough with stubble. I give him a sleepy smile as I'm still only half awake.

I barely stir as I feel his hands gently start to undress me. When I'm down to my panties, he hesitates, and then I feel him peel them off me. He runs his fingers in a sensual caress down my legs. I wiggle restlessly on the bed from the feelings his light touch ignites.

I suddenly feel his hot breath between my thighs and feel his tongue as he parts my folds. My eyes fly open, and I reach down and tug urgently on his hair.

He looks up at me with a wicked grin as he whispers, "Let me make you feel good, sweetheart."

I can only stare at him helplessly as he again bends his dark head and moves closer to my most intimate place. As he continues pleasuring me, I close my eyes and give in to the sensations. I start to pant as my body comes fully awake.

At one point, I reach down and impatiently pull his hair. I feel his amused smile against my inner thigh and feel the roughness of his unshaven face.

Then my body experiences the briefest of flutters, and suddenly, before I'm even ready for it, my body uncontrollably clenches, and I climax. I lose all thought as I just let go and give in to the feeling.

When I open my eyes again, I see a satisfied smirk on Michael's face. His gleaming green eyes rake appreciatively over my face, and he leans forward.

He whispers in a husky voice, "Go to sleep now, Honey. We'll talk in the morning."

Michael gently rises and then tucks in the covers around me, like I did earlier for the children. He walks to the door, and my eyes sleepily follow him. With his hand on the doorknob, he turns, and I see the regret etched on his face.

He states quietly, "I'm sorry I wasn't there for you tonight at dinner. I truly wanted to be."

Then he opens the door, and he's gone.

I roll over on my side as I snuggle into my pillow. I don't know how I feel about the situation anymore, but I fall asleep with a soft smile on my face.

Twenty

EARLIER THAT EVENING

Michael

Colleen pulls up to the imposing double security gates and rolls down her window.

She announces herself to the guards, "Colleen Kerry. I have Michael Garret with me. Vito granted him access to speak with Victor."

After a brief pause, the electronic gates creak open, and we drive through. Colleen parks in the estate's circular drive, and my eyes sweep over the perfectly manicured grounds. As we approach the stately front doors, they swing open silently, revealing a butler-turned-security guard. He gives us a cursory pat-down, and I feel an ominous shiver run down my spine as he checks my briefcase for weapons.

He then nods and says, "Follow me."

He leads us down an ornately decorated hallway. It reminds me of every Godfather movie I've seen, with its dark paneling and intricately carved woodwork that seems almost oppressive.

The man stops in front of a set of double doors and gives an abrupt knock.

"Colleen Kerry and Michael Garret to see Victor," he announces.

The doors swing open, and we step into a dimly lit room. Vito Mazarano sits in a high-backed leather armchair, his son Victor beside him. Behind them, two hulking bodyguards stand guard, their hands hovering near their weapons.

I take a seat on the elegant leather sofa, and Colleen sits beside me. Vito takes in our tense postures and gives an amused smile, but it lacks warmth. As the Mazarano men examine me, I return their gaze. Vito's eyes are cold and calculating, while Victor's seem more guarded.

I notice the electronic bracelet around Victor's ankle. It appears out of place against his elegant attire. He meets my gaze, his expression unreadable.

"I'm Michael Garret," I say quietly. "I've been hired to represent you in your murder case."

Victor nods calmly. "I'm sure you want to hear my side of the story."

"Yes," I reply. "I need to know exactly what happened that night."

I bend down, pick up my briefcase, and balance it on my knees. I glance up as the two bodyguards place their hands on their weapons.

"I'm just getting out a notepad and pen so I can take notes," I assure them.

I slowly click open my briefcase, get what I need, and close the lid. I turn toward Victor, feeling it's best if I just concentrate on him and not his father or the threatening bodyguards.

Suddenly, Vito makes an impatient sound and stands.

In an impatient voice, he states, "You know my feelings about this, Victor. We'll do things your way for now." Vito then turns to me. "My son did not kill Frank Zappo. Unfortunately, Victor is naive and believes in the judicial system."

"And I take it you don't?" I ask, my voice steady.

Vito lets out a low chuckle. "No, I do not. But I'm willing to allow you to try." He pauses, his eyes narrowing. "If you cannot find the true murderer, then I will provide someone willing to confess to the deed."

Victor gives me a rueful grimace as Vito strides out of the room.

"My father is old school. He's used to doing things his way." He shrugs. "I'm putting my faith in your skills, Mr. Garret."

I nod. "It's going to be a long night," I warn him. "Let's begin."

By the time I finally got home, the sun was just beginning to peek over the horizon, and my thoughts were a jumbled mess from painstakingly going over every little detail of what happened the night of the murder. I didn't know when or if I would get another opportunity to speak with Victor again.

Entering the dark house, I headed straight for the stairs when a movement had me glancing at the sofa. When I spotted Honey, it stopped me in my tracks.

TWENTY

A weak beam of sunlight caught in her hair as I walked silently over to her. She was sleeping soundly. I stood there for a few moments, letting the stress of the evening dissipate as I drank in her soft beauty. She looked so peaceful, but I knew she had to be upset with me for being a no-show at dinner. She was already nervous about me meeting her family.

Bending down, I gently scooped her up in my arms to carry her to her room. Where I was going to leave her sleeping soundly, like any good gentleman would.

I blink my eyes against the blaring sun streaming in through my bedroom window. I push off the covers and sit on the side of the bed. After showering and throwing on some clothes, I make my way down to the kitchen and smile when I see coffee is already made.

Honey left it for me. I smile as an image of her face last night flashes through my mind. I grimace so much for being a gentleman. I think with a smirk. Instead, I was overcome with desire and ended up pleasuring her. At least I honored Honey's wishes by not sleeping with her until after the wedding.

A note from Honey is waiting for me on the counter. *'Michael, I'll be with my family until I pick up the children. I'll let you know what their dinner plans are. XXXOOO.'*

I smile at the Xs and Os. Before I can even think about breakfast, I pull out my phone and call my admin.

"Schedule a mandatory meeting with the team at two o'clock to go over the Victor Mazarano case," I instruct her.

I stride purposefully into the office that afternoon and head straight for the conference room. My team is already seated, their eyes turning toward me as I enter.

"I met with Victor Mazarano last night," I announce, walking over to the whiteboard. The entire team falls into a stunned silence behind me. "He gave me a full accounting of the night of the murder." I quickly write a list of tasks for each team member.

As I speak, I can hear the beginnings of excited whispers behind me. I turn to the team.

"I can tell you're eager to dive in, and I am, too. We finally have something to go on. Make sure your research is solid. Leave no stone unturned. We need to find something, anything that will exonerate our client. Even if that means finding the person who killed Frank Zappo," I state firmly.

TWENTY

I can feel their enthusiasm growing. "Who wants to coordinate with Jaxson's P.I. team?"

A few hands go up, but I quickly decide on Howard. "Make sure to tell Jaxson this is a top priority," I state firmly. "Any questions?"

My phone buzzes, and I glance down to see a text from Honey. I type in a quick line back. When I look up again, everyone is staring at me expectantly.

"Unfortunately, you'll be on your own today, as I have to leave early." I rub my hands together. "Okay, everybody! Let's get to work—I'm counting on you."

A sudden wave of apprehension washes over me. This case is going to be just as challenging as I had anticipated. But with the determination and talent of my team, I believe we can turn things around. In fact, I'm counting on it.

"Dad? I didn't know you were going to be picking us up today!" Megan says in surprise as she climbs into the front seat.

I throw her a grin as I maneuver the SUV into traffic.

"I thought I'd save Honey a trip," I say easily.

Once we have Matthew, I drive to Skipper's house while the kids tell me about their day at school in between trying to describe all of Honey's family members. I have to laugh at some of their descriptions.

Honey meets us at the door with a wide smile. "You made it!"

I lean in, kiss her, and whisper, "Nothing was going to stop me today."

She takes my hand and pulls me with her as she walks to the covered terrace.

"Everyone, this is Michael," she announces in a steady voice.

I nod as her family gathers around. Honey then pulls me over to an older man.

I stick out my hand. "Mr. Mitchell?"

He nods, and I feel his eyes as they study me. I meet his gaze steadily.

"Glad you could make it today," he says as he shakes my hand firmly.

"Me, too. I apologize that I wasn't able to make it yesterday," I say sincerely. "Your daughter means a lot to me, and I wouldn't want to disappoint her or her family."

He nods and gives me a welcoming smile. "Call me Ezra," he states. Then he turns and introduces me. "Michael, this is my father, Honey's grandfather. Brian and his caregiver, Lock."

I solemnly shake their hands as Honey stands beside me with a soft smile.

Her grandfather nods and says quietly, "We understand you couldn't make dinner because of a murder case."

I grimace. "Yes, sorry about that. My client was finally available to meet with me."

Brian, Honey's grandfather, looks at me with shrewd eyes.

"Do you typically work with people like the Mazaranos?" He asks me point blank.

I blink, then decide to answer him truthfully. "Actually, no. I represented a man years ago, and he's the murder victim. I was... persuaded to accept this case at the last minute. I have my best team working on it right now."

I reach out, put an arm around Honey, and pull her closer.

"But my top priority will always be my family," I assure them as I smile down at Honey.

Twenty-One

Honey

"Honey, you look beautiful," I hear my oldest sister, Savannah, say as she carefully gives me a hug.

Georgia Ann steps up and says, "You're practically glowing!"

I smile at them as they step back so I can look at myself in the mirror.

I give a teary smile at my reflection. My hair is swept into a low chignon at the back of my head, with a few tendrils curling around my face. I have a few sprigs of baby's breath tucked into my hair, and I'll be carrying a bouquet of small white roses.

The girl in the mirror looks radiant—like a confident bride. A woman who loves and knows she's loved back. I blink as I wish that were true. But I've made my choice... for better or for worse, I chose a life with Michael. This is what I want.

With a wide smile, I turn to Megan and Paige. "You two look stunning in your dresses."

Paige smiles as she comes over and takes my hands. "I hope you and Michael will be as happy as Trent and I."

"Thanks. That means a lot," I tell her with a watery smile.

Megan then approaches with a delighted smile. "I can't wait for you to be my stepmom."

I reach out and gather her into a hug.

Aunt Skipper glances at the clock. "Okay, we need to get this show on the road. They should be starting the music any time now."

Right then, we hear the soothing sound of a harp. That's our cue, and we head down the stairs.

My father blinks the sudden moisture from his eyes when he sees me in my wedding gown.

TWENTY-ONE

I hang back while the rest of the girls walk out to the terrace. My sisters and aunt turn and wave to me and my father before disappearing into the array of white chairs on the lawn. Paige and Megan get into position. They are first down the aisle.

I turn to my father and smile. His face fills with pride and love as he takes my hand and places it over his arm.

He then turns and gives me a direct look. "It's not too late to back out if you have any doubts—"

My father stops talking when I immediately shake my head. I give him an earnest look.

"I love him, Dad," I say simply.

He searches my face and then gives me a smile filled with affection.

"I understand. You look at him the same way your mother looked at me," he states gruffly as he pats my hand gently.

We both turn as we hear the gentle, ethereal melody of the wedding march from the harp. It wafts through the air like a soft breeze. My father proudly leads me down the aisle toward my future husband.

A sweet, floral scent fills the air with a delicate fragrance, but I'm only vaguely aware as I feel locked in a bubble of joy as my eyes find Michael's. His vivid green eyes gleam with a happiness that fills me with hope as he holds out his hand to take mine.

The preacher begins the ceremony, and Michael and I pledge our holy vows to one another—our voices clear and steady. I send up a silent prayer of my own, asking God to bless our union.

I hear the preacher state, "You may now kiss the bride."

Michael beams as he carefully takes me into his arms and softly kisses me.

My heart soars when the preacher announces, "I now pronounce you husband and wife."

The reception proceeds in a blur of joyous emotions. Dancing with my father and grandfather is bitter-sweet. Then Michael takes me into his arms for our first dance.

He grins down at me and whispers, "I knew we'd move together well."

That's all he says, but his implied words have me blushing as he gently sways with me on the dance floor.

We've cut the cake. I've thrown the bouquet to Savannah with a playful grin, and the garter was caught by a friend of

TWENTY-ONE

Michael's. My aunt has now ordered me upstairs to change so Michael and I can leave on our honeymoon.

She and Paige trail behind me up the stairs. They assist me out of my wedding gown and into my traveling clothes. Our packed luggage is already in the car.

There's suddenly a tentative knock on the bedroom door. My aunt opens the door, and I see Michael's cousin, Mary, who is taking the children during our short honeymoon away. She gives me a hesitant smile as she enters the room.

Mary holds out an envelope and states softly, "I wasn't sure if now was the right time to give you this." Her eyes fill with sadness. "It's a letter from Michelle, Michael's late wife. She asked me to deliver it if Michael ever married again."

I hold out my hand for the letter. I glance down at it and then up at Mary.

"Thank you," I tell her with a sincere smile, feeling my heart begin to pound heavily in my chest.

I reach out, hug her, and then she leaves, softly closing the door behind her.

I'm left alone, as my aunt says quietly, "Paige and I will give you a few minutes of privacy."

I hear the click of the door closing as I sink onto the bed. I look at the feminine handwriting on the envelope that states simply, *'To: Michael's new wife.'*

I take a deep, fortifying breath and then open the letter with trembling hands.

> *'To the new Mrs. Garret,*
> *I'm very grateful that Michael has found you.*
> *Please know that I wished for him to marry again.*
> *I hope you are someone who makes him laugh, supports him, and loves him unconditionally, as that's all I ever wanted for him and my children.*
> *Don't worry about trying to fill my shoes. I know that Michael loves me. But that doesn't mean he can't love you, too. Michael loves deeply, fully, and with all his heart.*
> *He will be a wonderful and faithful husband.*
> *I'm happy for you both.*
> *Thank you for bringing joy back into his life.*
> *I could never hate or be jealous of the woman who helps Michael to heal.*
> *You're the best thing that could have happened to him.*
> *Sincerely and with love, Michelle Garret'*

TWENTY-ONE

I sit there staring at the letter until the words blur from the tears welling in my eyes. I look up when there's a soft knock on the door, and my aunt and Paige peek in.

"Are you okay?" Paige whispers.

I nod with a sniffle, and they come in. I hand them the letter with a gentle smile. They read it with solemn faces. I watch as they, too, blink back tears.

"Wow. That's some letter," Paige murmurs as they both envelop me in a warm hug. As we pull apart, Paige states, "I'd want to put a hex on the person replacing me."

My aunt and I both give a soft chuckle at Paige's obvious attempt to lighten the mood.

Aunt Skipper places her hands on my shoulders and states firmly, "That's a beautiful letter, Honey." Then she grins. "Come on now, let's see you smile. A bunch of people downstairs want to send the happy newlyweds off in style."

Paige laughs. "And the children can't wait to throw birdseed at you and their father."

As we descend the stairs, I see Megan and Matthew talking to their dad. Mary and her husband are behind them. Mary meets my eyes, and I give her a grateful smile. Then Michael turns and holds out his hand to me.

After we've all exchanged hugs and I've bid everyone farewell, we're ready to make a mad dash to the car, dodging the wildly thrown birdseed.

Before we jump inside, we turn and wave goodbye. I laugh as I shake the seeds out of my hair. Once in the car, I turn toward Michael, and he asks warmly, "Are you ready to start your life as Mrs. Michael Garret?"

I give him a brilliant smile as I nod and settle back in my seat.

We talk softly on the forty-five minute drive to the Ritz Carlton Hotel in Amelia Island. My eyes widen when we're shown to the luxury suite on the top floor.

The light is just beginning to fade as I glance out the floor-length glass doors leading to the two balconies overlooking the ocean.

Michael smiles as he opens the door so we can hear the sound of the surf in the background.

As I step onto the balcony, I murmur, "It's a beautiful view."

TWENTY-ONE

I turn to find his green gaze smoldering with a possessive desire as he looks at me. The look in his eyes suddenly makes it difficult to breathe.

"Yes, it is," he says in a husky voice. His eyes never leave mine. Suddenly, the walls seem to close in as he approaches me with a determined stride.

He steps out on the balcony and pulls me into his arms. His kiss starts off slow and savoring, but within a matter of minutes, it turns almost primal with his desire. I give a small whimper as his broad hands grip my backside and squeeze. He rubs me against his hardness.

Michael slowly starts to undress me. With each piece of clothing he removes, he tosses it behind him and into the hotel room. He continues until I'm standing in front of him naked, with only the gentle breeze from the ocean as covering.

The cool air caresses my exposed breasts, and I gasp as Michael's warm hands cup them. He rolls my nipple between his thumb and forefinger with one hand while he bends to cover my other breast with his hot mouth.

I'm swimming in a kaleidoscope of sensations as he continues to nuzzle against me. When he lifts his lips away from me, the cool breeze makes goosebumps rise on my skin. I shiver at the sensation left by his warm, wet mouth and the dry, cool breeze. I'm suddenly awash in the contrasts, and I give a soft moan when he finally wraps his hands around my waist and urgently picks me up.

I wrap my legs around his waist, and he carries me inside to the king-sized bed.

Twenty-Two

Michael

I hurriedly pull back the covers and set Honey down atop the silky sheets. Her eyes follow my movements as I quickly divest myself of my clothes. She watches silently as my hard cock proudly springs free.

Honey's eyes take in my engorged manhood and then dart to my face, which feels tight with my arousal. I never slow as I crawl over her and slide purposefully between her thighs. I spread her legs wider with my knees and enter her in one powerful stroke.

I still only after I'm inside of her. My green eyes blaze with my passion as I lift her face to mine. I cover her mouth, plunging deep, and I only begin to move after I raise my head from the kiss.

I pull half out of Honey's wet core and then surge back in. My lovemaking is rough, yet the rhythm I set is smooth. I grab her leg and pull it up and over my hip, giving me a different angle. As I continue to pump into her, I can tell I'm hitting that special spot inside of her, the one that makes her moan softly as her passion climbs.

Honey's eyes meet mine, and her amber eyes are ablaze with emotions. I feel my face harden even further with my desire, and my jaw clenches.

"Come for me, Honey," I demand in a guttural voice.

And she does. She's suddenly flying as her body takes over and spasms uncontrollably. I immediately follow her in my own release. Afterward, I gently hold her as our breathing slows.

I murmur in pleased satisfaction against her hair, "You're now mine."

I wrap my arm around her and pull her close. I hear Honey give a little sigh as she snuggles up against my chest.

"Yes, I'm yours," I hear her whisper back before we fall asleep, securely held in each other's arms.

TWENTY-TWO

When I wake up, it's still dark outside, but the breeze off the ocean has grown colder. I stand and walk nude to the balcony and shut the sliding glass doors. When I turn and walk back to bed, a moonbeam casts a golden glow over Honey's face. She's pulled the sheet up to cover her body, but one perky-tipped breast remains uncovered.

As my eyes rake over the globe of her lush breast, my body starts to harden. My gaze remains on her dusky pink areola and nipple as my need for her rises.

I greedily lower my head and take her nipple between my lips. I lightly bite down on it as Honey stirs restlessly in her sleep.

My hand slips under the sheet covering her body and zeros in on her moist heat. I lightly run my fingers through her folds, exploring her softly. As her eyes flutter open, I lean down and kiss her until she's fully away. As she returns my kiss, I probe a blunt finger through her now wet folds and slowly enter her, pushing high inside.

As I continue to kiss her mouth, I begin to pump my finger into her, then insert another. I pull slightly away from her mouth so I can plunge my fingers deeper into her welcoming heat. She moans as I go knuckle deep, and I don't let up as I continue to fuck her with my fingers.

She starts to buck against my hand as her passion swiftly builds. I don't stop as I can tell she's close. So, close.

As I curl my fingers slightly, adding just a bit more pressure, I whisper, "That's it, baby. That's it."

Then I press down firmly on her clit, and Honey shatters in my arms with a low keening cry. I continue to work her even through her orgasm.

When she's quieted, I pull her into my arms and whisper, "You're beautiful, Honey."

She gives a sleepy smile, but without opening her eyes, she settles against me and again falls asleep. I gently hold her soft form and listen to her slow and steady breathing.

My mind wanders to my last honeymoon and my wedding night with Michelle... My life was so different then. I was just beginning my career as an attorney. I was broke. We got married in a church, and her parents helped pay for the cake. I scraped up enough money to pay for the preacher and rent the reception hall.

For our wedding night, we went to our rental apartment instead of a fancy hotel. The apartment contained second-hand furniture and one queen mattress on the floor.

TWENTY-TWO

The electricity should have been turned on, but it wasn't. Michelle lit candles and placed them randomly around the rooms... we ate pizza delivery while she sat cross-legged on the bed, wearing one of my T-shirts.

Honey stirs in my arms. A feeling of guilty unease slides through me when I glance down at her. I shouldn't be thinking of my past life with Michelle while I hold Honey in my arms, even if it is devoid of emotion. It still feels like a betrayal to Honey.

A sigh escapes my lips as I gently loosen my hold on her and quietly get out of bed. I walk to the balcony in the other room, silently open the glass sliding doors, and step out. I glance back into the bedroom to make sure I didn't wake Honey. She's still sleeping peacefully.

I walk naked to the railing and lean my hands against it. Feeling the coolness of the metal against my palms. I lift my face silently to the darkened sky and focus on the ocean breeze—the slightly salty tang in the air. I open my eyes and stare blankly out at the unseen waves. I can hear the sound of the surf as it crashes against the shore, but my inward thoughts have my full attention.

I'm filled with a restlessness that I can't name. I honestly don't know what I'm feeling right now. I'm a mix of conflicting emotions. It's my wedding night... and I should be feeling something—right? Instead, I feel strangely numb, almost detached.

What should I be feeling now that I've made Honey my wife?

Desire? Absolutely! But love?

I care about Honey... I want her in my life and my bed. It's selfish, I know. But do I love her? I close my eyes as I honestly can't answer that question right now.

I just can't see myself ever opening my heart again to the wrenching pain of loss... I barely survived losing Michelle—I can't go through that type of pain again. I won't.

Besides, I like what I have with Honey. Physical attraction, companionship. She's a wonderful stepmother to my children. We're a family... Our life together will be good. She'll want for nothing - I'll make sure of that. But I won't give her *all* of my heart. I can't let it be broken again. Even if that means guarding my heart against her...

When I blink open my eyes, I see the sky isn't quite as dark. Dawn is fast approaching. I'm suddenly aware of the chill, of the slight dampness in the air coming in off the ocean. I turn and walk into the suite. I silently close the glass doors.

TWENTY-TWO

I slip back into bed and pull the covers over me, making sure Honey is covered. I don't pull her toward me as my skin still feels chilled. I lie on my back and close my eyes until sleep claims me.

When I open my eyes again, the room is filled with bright sunlight. I turn my eyes away from the glare coming in through the glass doors. I sit up in bed and glance around the bedroom, not seeing Honey. I stand and go into the other room but don't see her.

I use the main bathroom and then walk over to the cold coffee pot. As I reach for the pouch of coffee, I hear the sound of splashing water. I grin as I immediately turn and head toward the en suite bathroom.

As I turn the corner, I see Honey relaxing in the large stand-alone tub. She has her hair piled on top of her head. Her eyes are closed and she's wearing nothing but a contented smile on her face. The tub is filled with bubbles, and the air carries a light honeysuckle scent.

I smirk as I silently approach the tub. Her eyes fly open when I step into the water, avoiding her legs. She grins as she sits up, and I maneuver around behind her.

"Good morning," I murmur softly as I sit down in the warm water.

Honey sounds almost shy as she says, "Morning, I didn't mean to wake you."

She settles back against my chest with a deep sigh. The fragrant bubbles play peek-a-boo with her breasts. My hands immediately zone in on them as I cup each one, and my thumbs graze over her wet nipples.

Honey leans back even more and welcomes my touch as I gently play with her body. I nuzzle softly against the graceful curve of her neck and nibble on her earlobe.

She leans her head to the side, giving me more access and I immediately take advantage as my lips skim her soft skin. There's no sense of urgency this morning. We have plenty of time.

I whisper in her ear, "Do you like that?"

She smiles and murmurs, "Ah huh," and I see her lips curve up in a smile.

I grab a washcloth and lather it up with one of the provided soaps. I slowly drag it across her skin.

TWENTY-TWO

I take my time as I clean every part of her, enjoying the discovery of every freckle and tan line.

"I have all day to savor the taste and feel of you," I murmur against her neck, and I watch her shiver at my words.

She then turns and gets on her knees and slowly washes me, exploring my body. I grin lazily at her. As her touch turns bolder, I abruptly sit up. Her eyes widen in surprise.

"I'm trying to be a gentleman this morning. I don't want to make you sore," I explain.

She gives me a smile as her face turns a pretty pink. I stand and assist her out of the tub. I grab each of us a towel, and we slowly dry each other's bodies.

Wanting to avoid the temptation of the bed, I suggest, "How about we grab some breakfast and spend the rest of the morning at the beach?"

Twenty-Three

Honey

Michael takes my hand as we walk the trail from the hotel over the dunes. It's a beautiful day. The sun is bright, and there's hardly a cloud in sight. The sky is a clear, azure blue.

There are lounger chairs already set up along the sand. I follow Michael as he walks a little farther away from other guests. I'm surprised that it isn't more crowded as my eyes wander over the chairs and the small handful of people.

He turns and arches an eyebrow at me, and I nod. "This is perfect."

TWENTY-THREE

He hands me a towel, and I spread it over the lounger. I take off my swim wrap and smile as I feel Michael's eyes rake over me with an appreciative grin.

"Is that a new swimsuit?" He asks me. "I don't recall seeing you in that before."

I nod. "Yes, it is. Do you like it?"

"Oh, yeah. You look stunning in a bikini."

His gaze practically burns as his eyes rove over my body, missing nothing. The bikini is new, and I purchased it when he told me we would be honeymooning at the beach. It's a bright orange with gold accents. The way the suit flatters my curves makes me feel sexy, and Paige told me I had to buy it. She was right. Michael certainly seems to like the way I look in it.

I reach into my beach bag and pull out the suntan lotion.

"Here, let me," Michael says easily, reaching for the bottle. "Lay down, and I'll get your back."

He pushes the chairs into a reclining position, and I lie down on my stomach.

I feel his broad hands as he rubs the lotion into my back. He massages my shoulders and then moves lower. I love the feel of his strong hands as he continues to apply the lotion to my upper body. Then he moves to my legs. I tense as I feel his hands on my thighs. Michael thoroughly covers every inch of my exposed skin with the coconut-scented lotion, not missing a spot.

By the time he moves to my calves, I feel like a quivering bowl of jelly. I try to relax into the cushions as I feel his fingers gently massage my ankles, and then I feel his lips on my back as he lightly kisses me.

Michael reaches into the beach bag, pulls out a bottle of water, and places it within easy reach. He opens one and takes a long swig. I've curled to the side so I can watch his throat as he drinks. He's so masculine and strong. I feel a flutter in my belly as I continue to run my gaze possessively over my new husband.

I see a flash of white teeth as he gives me a knowing grin. He likes it when I look at him, so I don't move my eyes away.

As he lies down on his chair, I stand and pick up the suntan lotion. I pour some onto my palm and then sit on the edge of his chair. He moves over to give me more room, our thighs touching.

As I run my hands, which are slick with lotion, over his broad shoulder, his skin already feels hot from the bright sun overhead. I massage the lotion lovingly, moving my hands slowly from his shoulders down his ropy arms, feeling his biceps.

When I rub the lotion onto his back, I feel his muscles bunch underneath my palms.

"You're so muscular," I whisper to him as I continue rubbing the lotion down to his waist. I stop and pour more lotion out of the bottle. I start at his thick thighs, feeling his hair roughened skin as I carefully cover him with the sunscreen. Even his calves feel firm beneath my fingers as I run my hands lightly over his skin until I finally reach his ankles.

I frown as I look down at Michael. He hasn't moved since I started slathering him with the lotion.

"Michael?" I question with a slight frown.

He remains face down as he mutters, "Yeah?"

"Are you okay?"

"Yes. I just can't turn around right now," he says in a rough voice. "I like your hands on me a little too much."

"Oh," I mumble as understanding dawns. "Sorry about that." I give an unrepentant grin.

I stand and crawl onto the lounge chair beside him.

After a few minutes, I feel his arm reach out, and his fingers lightly trace the curve of my back.

"Don't be," he whispers.

A contented smile spreading across my face is my only response. We doze there for a few hours in the sun. I roll onto my back, the sun warming my skin. I reach for the sunscreen and apply it to my skin.

At Michael's raised brow, I shrug. "I like your hands on me as well, but I think it's safer if I do my front."

When I hand him the bottle, he takes it from me with an arrogant smirk that makes me laugh.

Michael stands and holds out his hand. "Come on, let's go for a walk."

I take his hand and follow him toward the surf. As we stand there watching the ocean, I feel the cool sand between my toes and the refreshing spray of the waves. The sound of the ocean is a constant rhythm, a soothing heartbeat.

We turn and walk slowly south, my hand still in his. The sun feels warm on our skin, and the breeze is gentle. I can't help but feel a sense of peace and contentment.

TWENTY-THREE

After a few minutes, Michael starts to talk, sharing some of his plans for the future.

"You already know that I'm a senior partner at the firm. The founding partners are very generous. All the partners get a percentage of the law firm's revenue."

I nod at his words. He turns to me and gently traces my cheek with his fingers.

"I'm trying to tell you that I've got a lot of money. The law firm makes over six hundred million a year. So, I'm pretty much set for life between what I bring in and with a percentage of their revenue."

My eyes widen in astonishment. "I knew you were well off. But I didn't know you were that rich," I tell him, my tone sincere.

He states proudly, "That's why I'm telling you now. You and the baby will never want for anything."

I give an inward grimace at his words. I've had no worries about money. My only concern is Michael's love for me.

He gives me a direct look and states, "If you want to hire a housekeeper or a nanny after this child is born we can easily afford it."

"Thank you, but I like doing things for the family."

As Michael frowns, his gaze tinged with doubt, I admit, "After the baby is born, I might consider having someone come in to clean, but I don't think I'll ever need a full-time housekeeper."

His look turns satisfied as he turns and begins to walk us back toward the chairs.

"I had no idea criminal law was so lucrative," I confess with a sheepish smile.

Michael laughs. "It isn't."

As I give him a confused look, he explains, "Criminal attorneys don't typically make a lot of money. However, the firm's founders strove from the beginning to build a glowing reputation. They only hire the best." He gives me a proud grin. "That's why so many interns come to work there. There's a lot to learn. Morgan Daniels and I, the other senior partner, are very selective in our clients. We also do a lot of pro bono cases as well."

As the rows of lounge chairs come into sight, my steps slow.

"Michael, can you tell me about the case you're working on now?"

His smile disappears in a flash. "Not now." He looks up and shrugs. "We're on our honeymoon, and I don't want to spoil our time together."

I give him a soft smile. "But you'll tell me later? Once we get back?"

He searches my eyes and then states quietly, "Yes. When we get back, I'll tell you what I can."

The look in his eyes sends a sense of unease flowing through me.

"Hey, It'll be okay. I just don't want anything to intrude. This is our time. No kids, just you and me."

He rubs his thumb over the back of my hand, and that touch is all it takes to make all my girly parts tingle.

"Thanks for telling me more about yourself and your work, Michael," I say with a wide smile. "When I first met you, my impression was that you were a gentleman. Intelligent and kind. I'm glad to know I'm right."

He cocks an eyebrow at me. "A gentleman?" His eyes get a wicked glint. "No, Honey. I assure you I am not a gentleman."

The hot look in his eyes steals my breath.

When we reach the lounge chairs, Michael picks up our towels and shoves our things into the beach bag.

He turns to me with a sly grin. "We're going back to the room."

A shiver runs through me at the almost primal hunger in his hot gaze.

Twenty-Four

Michael

I glance at my watch. It's almost time for us to check out. My smile widens into a smirk as I think back over our time together here at Amelia Island. We've spent a few hours at the beach each day and even dined out once. However, the majority of our time has been spent in the suite.

Getting to know each other so intimately was great. I love my children dearly, but I certainly haven't missed them on this trip, I think, with a smirk. Honey and I stopped to purchase a few trinkets for them at one of the shops when we left the hotel on one of those rare occasions.

I'll remember our special time here; we loved the luxury suite. There's a bench on the balcony that came in quite handy, I think, with a fond smile—remembering how Honey looked when I bent her over it and had my way with her. When she got loud from her desire, I had to cover her mouth to keep other guests from hearing what we were doing on the balcony.

I thought that after repeatedly making love to Honey, it would slake my desire, but instead, it seems to have increased my need for her.

I glance up as Honey walks out of the bedroom.

She smiles and states, "I'm ready." Then she glances around. "I enjoyed our stay."

"I did, too," I reply, my voice husky. "Maybe we should come back sometime—for our anniversary."

I watch as a blush covers her face. "That would be nice," she says with a wide smile.

The trip home is filled with companionable silence. We're picking up the children first as it's on the way home.

As the kids settle into the back seat, they can't wait to tell us about their stay. I glance at Honey and we share a smile.

TWENTY-FOUR

"Dad, Honey! We had so much fun. They let us jump on their trampoline!" Matthew states, his voice filled with excitement.

Megan then chimes in. "We went to the movies! It was great." Her eyes are shining as she continues, "We shared a huge bucket of popcorn and ate candy!"

"Can we get a trampoline?" My son asks, and I can hear the eager hope in his voice.

Megan asks as well, "Yeah, Dad, the trampoline was pretty awesome."

I glance in the review mirror and say, "Maybe for Christmas, we'll have to wait and see."

After I stop the car in front of the house, everyone scrambles from the car.

"Everybody get your own suitcase," I remind them.

Megan and Matthew are already halfway to the door. They swing around and head back while I get the luggage out of the back. As we approach the door, Megan suddenly stops and turns to me with an expectant look on her face.

"What?" I ask her as I step forward and unlock the door.

She replies in a loud whisper, "Aren't you going to carry Honey?"

At my blank look, Megan frowns and hisses, "You know, like in the movies? The groom always carries the bride over the threshold."

My face clears, and I approach Honey with a playful look in my eyes. As I scoop her into my arms, she gives a lighthearted laugh and places her arms around my neck. As I carry her into the house, the children's cheerful laughter follows us inside.

When I loosen my hold, I gently stand Honey on her feet. She looks up at me with shining eyes and I can't help it. I lean down and give her a slow kiss.

"Welcome home, Mrs. Garret," I say in a low voice.

"Dad! Can you help me with my suitcase? The wheel is stuck!" Matthew's loud voice cuts through the intimate bubble that surrounds us. The mood broken, I turn with a grimace, and help him with the luggage.

As I place Honey's suitcase in the main bedroom I give a satisfied smirk. Starting tonight, Honey will share this room with me.

I hear Honey at the door.

TWENTY-FOUR

"Michael, should I..."

Her voice trails off as she stops and looks around the room with stunned surprise.

"When did you have the room redecorated?" she asks, her voice filled with shocked surprise.

I walk over and take her in my arms.

"I thought we deserved all new furniture," I say softly.

Honey looks around with a brilliant smile. "Thank you." Then, as her gaze roves over the room, she says with wonderment tingling in her voice. "How did you know I liked this style?"

"Remember when we were picking out a new dresser for Matthew? I heard you tell Megan you loved the way this bedroom set looked," I tell her with a grin. "Do you like the different shades of beige and brown?" I ask with a frown.

"I love it!" Honey says as she turns in a circle. "It's gorgeous! The lamps, the bed, and the comforter... It's perfect!"

As I reach for her, Megan comes barging through the door with her brother right behind her.

"Oh! I wanted to see Honey's face when she saw the new furniture," she says with a pout.

I smile at my daughter and state, "Honey was totally surprised. She said she loves it."

Megan finally grins. "I knew she would!" She turns toward Honey, "I told Dad you liked warm colors."

"You were right, Megan," Honey says as she gives Megan a quick hug. "Everything looks beautiful. It was a wonderful surprise."

"Megan and Matthew, Honey, and I brought back souvenirs from the beach for you guys. They're on the dining room table."

The words are barely out of my mouth before the kids race downstairs to find their gifts.

I turn to Honey with a rueful grin. "We need to start locking our bedroom door."

Before I left this house this morning, Honey reminded me of her doctor's appointment. When my phone buzzes that it's time for me to leave, I glance around at the hardworking group of young attorneys.

"Good work, team, finding these new leads." I give each of the team members a direct look. "Now, I need every one of these leads followed." I smile at their mild groans. "I know, I know.

Right now, I have to leave for an appointment, but I'll need a status report first thing tomorrow," I inform them.

With a nod, I leave the room and head home to pick up Honey.

After a brief wait, we're escorted to an examination room. A nurse has already taken Honey's vitals. We both look up as her doctor enters the room.

"Hello, Honey... Garret? Ah, I see congratulations are in order." The doctor smiles at Honey.

Then the doctor turns to me. "Mr. Garret, I'm Dr. Collins. I'm glad you were able to make it for the first ultrasound." She then states, "I'll talk to you both after the procedure. We can also go over any questions at that time."

The doctor gives us a friendly smile and then exits the room. I walk over to Honey and take her hand. The door opens, and the technician enters the room. I watch as the sonographer introduces herself and then smears goop on Honey's abdomen and performs the ultrasound.

I hold Honey's hand during the procedure. Afterward, while we wait for the results, I quietly pull a chair closer and give her hand a squeeze.

We both turn when the doctor comes in.

"I've just finished going over the results. The fetal heartbeat is normal, and the baby appears to be developing fine," the doctor smiles. The doctor gives us the due date and then asks, "Any questions for me?"

I raise my eyebrows at Honey, and she shakes her head. The doctor looks at us in surprise.

"No questions? That's unusual," she states bluntly.

"I have two children: a ten-year-old daughter and a seven-year-old son," I reply with a grin. Then I look down at Honey. "But this is Honey's first child. Are you sure you don't have any questions?" I ask my wife with a slight frown.

Honey looks from me to the doctor. "I read all of the pamphlets I was given. If I think of something later, can I call your office?"

"Of course," the doctor replies. Then she turns back to ask, "Mary Catherine, I believe you said you were a nanny. Will you be continuing to work full-time?"

Honey and I both give a soft chuckle.

I clear my throat and state, "Doctor, I was a widower, and Honey took care of my children."

The doctor nods. "Oh, I see," she states with a twinkle in her eyes. "So, you'll still perform the same job as their stepmother."

Honey nods as a blush spreads across her cheeks. "Yes, I guess that's right," she says with a widening smile.

As the doctor turns to leave, I glance down at Honey and say playfully. "I wonder if they get a lot of nannies in here."

The doctor turns around with a grin and states drily, "You'd be surprised. I think the Sound of Music started a trend."

Twenty-Five

Honey

"Mrs. Garret! Yoo Hoo, Mrs. Garret!"

I hear someone calling my name as I approach Megan's cheerleading practice and turn around.

"Yes, I'm Mrs. Garret," I tell the slightly out-of-breath stout woman as she hurries toward me.

"Oh, good. Your daughter, Megan, signed up for Girl Scouts, and I need a parent's signature."

"Megan's my stepdaughter," I reply. "I didn't know she was interested in signing up."

TWENTY-FIVE

"We had a sign-up booth at the school last week," the woman explains.

"I see. Okay, I'll discuss this with her father. When do you need it back?"

The woman grimaces as she pushes a stray curl behind her ear.

"I'm sorry, we need the form signed today." She gives a slight frown and then mumbles, "I was hoping Megan had already mentioned this to you and her father, but you know kids."

She shrugs. "Just the other day, my son Jeffrey completely forgot he needed cupcakes and…" Her voice trails off as she bites her lip. "Sorry, you probably have to be somewhere and I tend to rattle on."

I can't help but smile at the woman's bubbly personality.

"I was a Senior Girl Scout," I say right as Megan comes hurrying over; her practice must have finished.

"Hi, Honey and Mrs. Smith." Megan starts to smile, and then her eyes widen. "Oh no. I completely forgot about the form."

Before I can say anything, the older woman assures her, "That's okay, Megan. No worries, someone at the office pointed out your stepmom."

Megan gives a relieved smile. "Good! Honey, can you sign for me to join?"

I bite my lip. "I really should run this by your father first…" I trail off as I try to decide the best course of action.

Mrs. Smith states in a persuasive voice, "This year, the troop meetings are directly after school and across the street at the church. So, all the girls can walk to the meetings, which will be nice for the parents as you'll only have to pick them up."

I look from her to Megan, undecided. Finally, I nod. "Alright. Since it's due today, I'll go ahead and give approval."

Mrs. Smith hands me the form, I sign it and hand it back. She smiles as she tucks the form in her folder and then hands me some papers.

"Thank you, Mrs. Garret. Here's a list of things Megan will need. Since you were a Girl Scout, I'm sure you're familiar with everything on the list."

Megan turns toward me in surprise. "Honey, you were a Girl Scout?"

I nod. "Yes, a Senior Scout, and my mother was a Girl Scout leader when I was growing up," I say with a bit of pride.

TWENTY-FIVE

Mrs. Smith gives us a delighted smile. "Well, then. I hope you'll consider being active with our troop." Her eyes fairly sparkle with enthusiasm.

"I'll think about it, Mrs. Smith," I promise the woman.

She gives Megan and me a cheery wave, and then she disappears around the corner.

Megan says, "Thanks, Honey. I totally forgot about the form."

"We'll let your dad know at dinner," I tell her as we head toward the car to pick up Matthew.

That night, after dinner and dessert, we begin to clear the plates. Megan stands up when I glance at her and then nod my head toward her father.

"Dad, I signed up for Girl Scouts last week when you guys were away. I forgot to bring the form home for you to sign—"

Michael interrupts her with a firm statement, "Megan, bring home the form. I'll read it over, and we can discuss it then."

Megan says eagerly, "That's okay, Dad. Honey already signed it. We just wanted you to know." Then, with a wave, she runs lightly up the stairs.

Matthew turns to me, "Honey, can you help me with my math homework later?"

"Sure," I say vaguely, with my eyes on Michael, who has stiffened, an unreadable look across his face. "Matt, why don't you go upstairs and start on your homework for now?"

With a carefree shrug and nod, he bounds up the stairs.

Michael turns to me, his face expressionless. "You signed Megan up for something without talking to me first?"

"Yes, but—"

"Honey, you're their stepmother now, but you should have waited to ask me," he says in a tight voice.

"I know, but you see—"

He abruptly stands. "I was thinking of you when I told Megan we'd discuss it. You'll be busy with the new baby. You won't have time to run Megan to meetings."

"Michael, the Scout leader, said the deadline was today." When I open my mouth to explain further, he abruptly turns away. My heart begins to pound with a mixture of anger and frustration.

"Don't turn away from me. We were having a discussion," I sputter in disbelief, my voice trembling slightly.

He halts and then slowly turns around. "You already made the decision for me, so there's nothing to discuss."

My eyes go wide, then narrow at him in exasperation. "Michael, I'm not a child, and I'm not your employee any longer." I place my hands on my hips. "I'm your wife, and I want to discuss this."

Michael frowns and states, "You say you're not a child, yet you're acting like one." He raises his brow at me. "Tonight, I don't have time to hash this out. You've already signed the form without even asking me about it. You can't void them, now."

I stare at him as I feel a surge of irritation. I'm trying to be understanding, but he's being unreasonable. I take a deep breath and try to calm down.

In a softer voice, I state, "I just want us to have a conversation about this."

Michael shrugs and states wearily, "Honey, I have important files I need to go over tonight. Quite frankly, I don't have time to pander to your wishes. I have work to do."

With those parting words, he turns and walks away.

A lump forms in my throat as I watch Michael disappear around the corner. I feel a wave of anger and disappointment wash over me and tears well in my eyes. I clench my fists and take deep breaths to keep my emotions in check as I finish wiping down the table. I guess the honeymoon is definitely over, I think grimly.

I glance into the kitchen, and I suddenly don't care if there are dirty dishes in the sink. They can wait until I feel like doing them. I'm done.

I toss my hair, lift my chin, then paste a smile on my face, and walk upstairs to assist Matthew with his homework. It's not his fault that his otherwise reasonable father is acting the way he is.

After I help Matthew with his math, he shouts for Megan and we all walk downstairs. By mutual agreement, we enter the living room. Matthew sprawls on the carpet with a pillow, and Megan and I sit on the couch.

Matthew grabs the remote and turns it to our favorite show.

"Honey, can we have popcorn?" Matthew asks.

TWENTY-FIVE

With a nod, I stand and go into the kitchen. Megan trails behind me. I get down the popcorn and pop up two bags in the microwave. Megan helps me distribute it, but as she starts to pour some into the big bowl I normally share with Michael, I shake my head.

"Your father is working in his office tonight," I tell her with a grimace. "Let's not disturb him."

"Okay," Megan says as she fills three smaller bowls. "Did you go over the Scout schedule and list with Dad?"

I shake my head. "No, he's busy. We can go over the list with him another time," I say easily.

Megan grabs a handful of popcorn and shoves it in her mouth as we walk to the couch to watch the show.

By the kid's bedtime, Michael still hasn't shown himself. So, I head upstairs with the children. I undress, pull on a silky nightgown, and crawl into bed. I want to stew about how Michael acted, but instead, the minute my head hits the pillow, I fall asleep.

I groggily open my eyes when I feel Michael slide into bed. I feel his arm around my waist, and then his broad hands rub lightly over the silkiness of my nightgown. I instantly stiffen in his arms.

Then I yank away and glance over my shoulder at Michael, who's frowning.

"Why did you pull away from me?" He asks with a confused grimace, "Don't you like me touching you?"

I shoot a glare at him as I hiss, "Normally, but not when I'm still wanting to hit you over the head with something."

He blinks and mutters, "It's not good to go to bed, mad. I know we had a disagreement, but we're married. We should leave our grievances outside the bedroom door."

I quirk my eyebrow at him and demand, "Is that what you and Michelle did?"

"Yes," he says with an agreeable grin.

"Well, I'm not Michelle. And I don't want you touching me tonight!" I say in a huff, "You acted like a jerk, and I don't feel like even kissing you right now."

I then roll over with my back to him and pull the covers over me.

I can feel him studying me, trying to see if I mean what I'm saying.

He shifts his weight on the bed like he's reaching out for me.

TWENTY-FIVE

"Don't even think about it!" I say sharply.

I feel him hesitate but don't turn around; instead, I settle deeper into my pillow.

The next morning, before the alarm goes off, I carefully get out of bed without waking up the slumbering giant of a man beside me. I pull on some clothes and walk downstairs.

As the children are finishing their breakfast, Michael walks into the kitchen. I silently hand him his coffee mug.

"Thanks," he says warily as his eyes study my face. I don't look at him. I'm still fuming over the way he treated me. When he leans in for a kiss, I turn my head so his lips land on my cheek.

He dutifully places a kiss on the side of my face and then says carefully, "Have a good day, Honey."

"You too, Michael," I say breezily and then turn to the kids. "You guys ready to leave for school?"

They both nod, and I head out the door with Megan and Matthew without a glance in Michael's direction.

Twenty-Six

Michael

I stand there, stunned by Honey's cold indifference, as the door closes behind her and the kids. The kitchen is a mess; last night's dishes are still piled in the sink, and Megan and Matthew's cereal bowls are on the table.

I glance at my watch and begin stacking the dishes in the dishwasher. After wiping down the table, I turn on the machine and listen to the hum of the motor.

I realize I've only seen Honey angry twice before: the night we first made love and last night. Michelle, on the other hand, was quick to anger but equally quick to forgive. From what I can tell, Honey is slow to anger, but once she's mad... look out.

TWENTY-SIX

Honey hates dirty dishes left in the sink. This tells me just how upset she still is. I didn't handle the situation well last night. I wince as I think about how I acted. I was taken aback that Honey signed Megan up for something without even asking me... but did I have to be such an ass?

It suddenly hits me like a tidal wave—I never apologized to Honey.

Guilt and regret surge through me, and I know I have to make this up to her.

Yet, I feel out of my depth here. I knew how to apologize to Michelle, but last night and this morning have shown me that I need to brush up on my apology skills. I've gotten rusty, probably because Honey always did what I asked her to, but that was when she was my nanny. Now she's my wife. I wince again as I remember telling her she was acting like a child. Shit! No wonder she didn't want me touching her.

I stand there a few more minutes. I feel a bit lost and confused as I rub my chin, trying to figure out how to make it up to her. When my eyes land on the clock, I sigh. I need to get to work. It could take me all day for me to come up with a good apology anyway.

That afternoon I look up as my admin comes to the door. Seeing the uneasy look on her face, I lean back in my chair.

"Is Marcel and Bruno waiting to see me?" I ask her with a grimace. When she nods, I mutter in a resigned voice, "Show them in."

Marcel and Bruno enter, their presence filling the room with a palpable tension. They look a little too comfortable as they casually take a seat.

"Gentlemen, please make yourselves at home," I say drily.

Marcel narrows his eyes at me and asks, "How's the case coming along?"

"I submitted my weekly status report this morning," I reply in a flat voice.

"Yeah, well, about that. Vito Mazarano asked us to come down to remind you that if you can't find something soon, he can..." Marcel pauses with a smirk. "Let's say...offer up someone willing to take the fall."

I feel a cold sweat breaking out on my forehead. "My team and I are looking into every possible lead." I lean forward in my chair. "Please remind Mr. Mazarano that this is a high-profile case. Many eyes will be perusing the evidence. I don't mean just those in the courtroom. If false evidence is submitted, it will not further his son's cause."

Then I continue, "We have a couple more months before this case goes to trial. I need more time."

Marcel and Bruno give me a blank look, their eyes cold and calculating. I know it's meant to intimidate me, and I steel my resolve, but I can feel a knot tightening in my stomach at the thinly veiled threat behind their stares.

Marcel stands and raises his eyebrows at me. "I hope you know what you're doing, Garret."

The words, 'I do, too,' float through my mind as I watch them turn toward the door.

With his hand on the doorknob, Marcel turns around.

He states smoothly, "By the way, say hello to your family for me: your daughter, son, your new wife, and the baby."

Then he and Bruno slowly exit my office, their point made. I feel the sucker punch as my face goes pale. How do they know about the baby? Honey and I haven't told very many people. Even the children don't know. Yet these thugs were able to gather that information easily.

Vito Mazarano wanted me to be reminded that there is more at stake here than just his son. The threat to my entire family was clear and precise. I would be a fool not to take heed of his warning.

Unfortunately, I meant what I said. If I take Vito up on his offer and they find some poor schmuck to take the fall, the authorities would figure it out. They are watching this case very closely. It's not every day someone is granted bail for murder, even if the bail was significant at fifteen million dollars. A cynical smile spreads across my face, and I shake my head.

I glance up as Nancy comes to the door.

"I'm leaving early today, Michael. Is there anything you need me to do before I go?" she asks.

"Yes, Nancy," I nod and arch an eyebrow at her. "What does your husband do to apologize when he's been a total ass?"

When I get home, I can smell Honey's Thursday night pot roast the minute I open the door.

"Honey, it smells delicious in here," I say sincerely with a smile.

TWENTY-SIX

Honey nods in acknowledgment but doesn't turn around, her back stiff, so I head upstairs to our bedroom. I get a few things ready and then come back downstairs.

During dinner, the kids keep glancing from me to Honey with a puzzled look in their eyes. They can tell something isn't right between us.

After dinner, Matthew asks, "Honey, is their apple pie for dessert?"

"Not tonight," Honey says with a shake of her head.

Matthew gives me a confused look, then shrugs and starts clearing the table without being told. I notice Megan follows suit.

I go upstairs, fill the tub with bubbles, and light the scented candles I put out. I have the softest towels we have already laid out and placed invitingly by the tub. Honey's favorite music plays softly in the background. The melody soothing.

When I hear the kids come upstairs, I gesture for Megan to follow me. I step inside Matthew's room.

"I need your help. I want to surprise Honey with some alone time tonight. How about I take you guys to the town center for a couple of hours?"

Smiles spread across their faces.

"Sure!" Matthew says as his eyes go wide.

Megan says, "Can we go to Old Navy?"

I nod. "Yes. I want this to be a surprise, so I'm going to bring Honey upstairs, and then we'll leave, okay?"

I warily approach Honey and murmur, "Honey, can I talk to you? Upstairs?"

She swings around and narrows her eyes on me.

I shrug my hands and say, "I want to apologize."

Honey takes a deep breath and then gives me a curt nod. I follow her up the stairs and into our bedroom.

"Honey, I'm sorry. I acted without thinking things through last night. I know you only signed that form because you thought it was the best course of action. I'm sorry that I didn't give you the benefit of the doubt." I see her face slightly soften. "I won't let it happen again."

She gives me a hesitant nod, and I can tell she's willing to meet me halfway.

TWENTY-SIX

"Tonight, I'm taking the kids out for a few hours so you can have some alone time. I fixed you a bubble bath so you can relax undisturbed."

Honey's eyes get a pleased look, and her smile widens. I follow her as she peeks into the en suite and sees the candles and the full tub of scented bubbles.

She turns to me and says, "Thank you. Michael."

That's all, but I can tell the cold, icy wall that was between us has broken if not completely thawed.

Honey follows me out to the upstairs landing.

"Have fun," she calls down to the children with a wave and a smile.

Then I squeeze her hand and silently leave the house and Honey alone. I can only hope that my sincere effort to apologize will help Honey to forgive me.

Twenty-Seven

Honey

I lean back against the tub and let the warm, fragrant water soothe me. I smile softly, thinking of the sincerity in Michael's eyes when he apologized.

I lazily lift one arm out of the water and watch as droplets drizzle down my arm. I must say it feels heavenly to have the place to myself with nothing to do but relax.

My mind drifts back to last night. My feelings were deeply hurt when Michael questioned my signing the form for Megan. I was disappointed by how he acted, which, in turn, made me angry. I wasn't prepared for him to act so unreasonably.

I grimace; he's been under a lot of stress lately due to his new case. I could have been a bit more understanding as well. We were told in Home Economics class that marriage was a fifty/fifty type relationship. But they were wrong. It's more dynamic than that. Sometimes, you give ninety percent, and the other person only gives ten. Then that reverses, and you're the one only giving ten percent, but most often, things seem to work out.

I suddenly grin. A sincere apology and a hot bath never hurt, either. Now, I need to be willing to forgive him and not hold his grouchiness against him.

I settle back in the water with a sigh as the bubbles start to disperse. My mind goes over my time with Michael since we married. He's been wonderful. That's partly what shocked me when he acted unreasonably... but I know he was a single parent calling all the shots for the last two years. We're newly married, and it's going to take a bit of time before we get this co-parenting thing down pat.

As for the rest of our marriage... A shiver goes down my spine as I think about our sex life. Michael is an experienced and demanding lover. I get a dreamy look in my eyes as I think about him and how we shared a tub during our honeymoon.

After a few more minutes, I slowly blow out the candles and stand. I scoop up the towel Michael set out and wrap it around me. I do feel pampered.

I get out my favorite body lotion and slowly massage it into my skin. I decide to give myself a mani/pedi. I get out my nail polish and carefully paint my nails. As I sit there waiting for the polish to dry, I think about the baby. We discussed turning the spare bedroom into a nursery, and I can't wait to start decorating. We need to tell the children before too long before the baby starts to show.

I place my hand lovingly over my abdomen.

"I love you very much, little one. I hope you can feel my love," I whisper softly.

I slowly pull a nightgown over my head, slip into my robe, and pad downstairs. I curl up in an armchair and pull out my e-reader. Soon, I'm lost in a steamy romance. As I read, I can't help but picture Michael as the muscular and handsome hero...

When I hear their car doors slam, I close the lid on my e-reader.

Megan and Matthew come bounding through the front door with shopping bags and huge smiles on their faces. They're arguing good-naturedly about who has more packages than the other. Michael trails behind them with an indulgent look on his face. His hands are filled with packages as well.

Our eyes meet over the heads of the children, and I see a glimmer of relief flicker in his gaze as he returns my smile. He immediately comes over to me, leans down, and kisses me softly.

"You look nice and relaxed," he murmurs in a satisfied voice.

I smile up at him. "I feel pampered."

"Good. You deserve to be pampered," he says in a low voice.

"Honey! Look what I got!" Matthew excitedly comes over and proudly shows me a new game that his dad bought for him.

I lift an eyebrow at Megan, who has a large Old Navy shopping bag clutched in her hands.

She grins and says eagerly, "They had jeans and tops on sale. I got three new outfits."

I glance at Michael, who gives me a sheepish look. I just grin and continue to ooh and ah over the new items they show me.

I'm surprised when Michael announces it's the kid's bedtime. The time went by so quickly.

Before Megan runs upstairs, she turns and says, "Honey, I forgot to tell you. Guess who we ran into?" She grins. "Mrs. Smith, the Girl Scout leader, and her son Jeffery. She said to tell you hello."

Michael sighs as he sits down on the couch. He leans his head back against the cushions.

"I'd forgotten how rambunctious it is to shop with those two," he looks over at me with a rueful smile. "They wore me out."

I give a soft chuckle. "I understand how you feel."

Suddenly, his eyes turn serious. "Mrs. Smith is a big fan of yours."

"Really?" I say cautiously.

Michael nods. "Yes, she said she hoped you didn't feel too pressured into signing the form for Megan. She also told me you had wanted to run it by me first."

He grimaces. "She hopes you will consider helping out since you were a Scout and your mother was a Troop Leader."

I glance at Michael with a slight smile. "She's quite the bubbly personality. Isn't she?"

TWENTY-SEVEN

He winces. "She's a little overwhelming...but Megan seems to like her."

Michael hesitates and says, "I completely understand why you signed the form. Mrs. Smith is very... persuasive. She's also a talker. She kept us there for over twenty minutes."

I bite my lips to keep from laughing.

"After meeting her, I felt even more of a heel for how I acted. I really am sorry, Honey," Michael tells me. I can hear the heavy remorse in his tone.

I stand and then sit down beside him on the couch.

"I accept your apology, Michael," I tell him in a soft voice.

"Good," he says as he pulls me closer. I snuggle up against him. He reaches into the shopping bag at his feet and pulls out a brightly wrapped gift with an eager grin.

My eyes go wide in surprise, and I glance up at him.

"You've already apologized," I say quietly.

Michael smiles. "This isn't an apology gift." He urges softly, "Open it."

I take the wrapped package, and with a curious smile, I open it.

"Oh, Michael! It's for the baby! It's perfect!" I sniffle, overcome with emotion.

"Hey, I didn't mean to make you cry. It's our baby's first gift," he says with a soft gleam in his eye.

"It's so soft." I rub my cheek against the sweet, fluffy stuffed lamb.

"I couldn't decide which stuffed animal I wanted to buy, but then I saw this little lamb," he says in a low voice and sings, "Mary had a little lamb, little lamb, little lamb... Mary had a little lamb whose fleece was white as snow." He leans down and gives me a soft kiss.

Then he whispers, "I thought it was perfect for Mary Catherine's first child."

I give him a trembling smile. "I think it's the baby hormones that make me so emotional," I sniffle. "Thank you, Michael."

I look up at him and ask, "When do you think we should tell Megan and Matthew?"

He reaches down and covers my slight baby bump with a broad hand.

"This weekend?" he suggests.

I give a smile filled with happiness as I nod. As we climb the stairs later, Michael catches me in a huge yawn.

When we enter the bedroom, he crawls in beside me and gently takes me into his arms. He kisses me a chaste kiss and pulls my back against his chiseled chest.

He whispers, "You're exhausted. Go to sleep."

"I'm not that exhausted, Michael—" I argue, but he interrupts me with another kiss.

"Sleep. I promised myself I'd let you sleep and only hold you tonight," he whispers tenderly against my hair.

I snuggle my back up against him.

"Michael, I don't like it when we fight. It doesn't feel good," I say, my voice barely above a whisper.

"I agree, Honey," he says softly.

Then, with a faint sigh, I close my eyes and surrender to sleep.

When I blink my eyes open the next morning, the sun is just beginning to lighten the room. I'm still being held against Michael's chest. I listen to his steady breathing as I lie there contently in his arms.

After a few moments, I feel Michael stir behind me as he slowly wakens. I feel his hands slowly caress me through the silky fabric of my nightgown. The nightgown that has ridden high around my hips during the night.

I feel Michael's hardness behind me as it presses against the back of my thigh. I arch my back to rub against him. I feel him harden even more. I'm suddenly burning up with the need to feel Michael inside me.

With a sense of urgency, I deliberately rub against him, and I hear him catch his breath. His broad hands reach down and lift my nightgown higher as he presses his hips to mine.

He lifts my right knee so he can slide between my legs, and then he enters me from behind. His hands guide me as he sets a slow but steady rhythm as he begins to stroke into me. We remain spooned as he increases the pace of his thrusts. Soon, I'm panting as he pounds into me from behind.

Our lovemaking is silent except for our harsh breaths. When I finally reach that pinnacle and teeter on the edge, I feel Michael's hand as he thrums my clit, and then I'm lost in a flood of sensations. I reach a trembling climax as he hugs me tight.

TWENTY-SEVEN

Once I'm done, he takes over, and I continue to push back against him, meeting his eager thrusts. He gives a hoarse groan as he empties himself inside me.

He holds me against him, and we drift back to sleep, totally sated by our lovemaking.

Twenty-Eight

Michael

It's Saturday morning, and as we eat a hearty breakfast of hot, buttered blueberry pancakes, I clear my throat and take Honey's hand in mine.

"Megan. Matthew. Honey and I have an announcement," I say in a warm voice. "Honey's having a baby. You're going to have a little brother or sister."

Their eyes go round, and then each of them reacts.

"Really? Oh my gosh! Can I hold the baby once it's born?" Megan asks, her eyes shining.

Matthew says, "Cool! Will the baby be a boy?"

TWENTY-EIGHT

I answer, "Yes, Megan." I look at Matthew. "It could be a boy or a girl."

Matthew shrugs. "Okay, but I'd rather have a brother."

Honey and I share a grin at Matthew's words.

Megan is definitely more excited than my son, and she jumps up and hugs Honey.

"I can help with the baby!" she volunteers eagerly.

Honey smiles at my daughter. "I'm counting on it, Megan."

Megan continues to ask Honey questions as I stand and clear the table, allowing them to talk excitedly. Honey is practically glowing as she discusses the baby with Megan.

Honey's cell phone begins to buzz on the counter. Her Aunt Skipper's face flashes on the screen. I hand it to Honey.

"Hi, Aunt Skipper," she says, her voice filled with warmth. I idly listen in on the conversation as I move from the kitchen to the table.

"Tomorrow for dinner? Let me ask Michael." Honey glances at me with a raised eyebrow.

I shrug. "Sure, I don't have anything planned," I assure her.

That afternoon, Honey and I walk upstairs and check out the guest bedroom.

Sunlight streams through the window, casting soft shadows on the worn wooden floor.

"What would you like to do first?" I ask Honey.

"We need to get rid of the furniture..." She tilts her head and then goes over and sits down in the rocking chair.

The air in the nursery is still and quiet, save for the gentle creak of the chair. Honey sits there, her eyes closed, a peaceful smile playing on her lips.

"This can stay," she says with a pleased smile as she opens her eyes.

My eyes travel down her body, and I imagine her sitting there with a newborn in her arms. A surge of emotion travels through me, taking me by surprise.

"Michael?" Honey's voice pulls me back to the present.

I blink and clear my throat. "Sorry."

Honey smiles. "I'd like to have the walls painted. Maybe a soft yellow?"

TWENTY-EIGHT

She stands and walks toward me. I pull her back to rest against my chest as we survey the room again.

"Yellow works for a boy or a girl," I say softly.

"Since the rocking chair is white, I'm thinking we could add a white crib and maybe a dresser. Oh, and a changing table."

"I like all your ideas," I murmur as I sway with Honey in my arms. I gently reach around her and place my hands over her slight baby bump.

"I think there's some odds and ends in the closet. I can clear them out today," I promise her.

"Sure, there's no hurry." Honey bites her lip and says, "I'd like to get window treatments, just something to soften the look of the blinds."

I grin down at her and state, "Whatever you want, Honey. I know you'll make it a peaceful haven for the baby."

Honey looks up at me with shining eyes. "Yes, a peaceful haven... I like that."

We stand that way, both of us daydreaming about our future and our baby. I suddenly get a lump in my throat as I imagine my life with Honey a few years down the road.

"I already feel a deep love for our child, Honey," I admit in a whisper.

Honey's warm brown eyes gaze up at me, her expression filled with a mixture of love and yearning.

"I know you'll be a great mother," I assure her with a proud smile. "You already are a great mom to Megan and Matthew."

In a voice filled with gratitude, I say, "You helped my children get over the grief of losing Michelle. You're more than just a stepmother to them."

"What about you, Michael?" She asks me with a searching look filled with longing. "Am I more than their stepmother to you?"

"Of course," I say gruffly.

A feeling of unease sweeps through me, and I loosen my hold on her and clear my throat. I abruptly turn.

"You're a wonderful wife. You've strengthened our family unit." I avoid looking at the hurt in her eyes.

I state briskly, "We can plan a shopping trip to pick out the furniture and anything else you may want."

I turn and walk out of the soon-to-be nursery, the feeling of contentment shattered. I can't shake the feeling that I've let Honey down.

Right before six o'clock, we pile out of the SUV and ring the bell. Honey's aunt opens the door, her face beaming with a warm smile.

"Glad ya'll could make it," she states in her Southern drawl. "I thought we'd eat outside."

The kids, who are now familiar with the house, race toward the terrace, their laughter echoing through the air. Honey and I follow at a more leisurely pace.

"Aunt Skipper, do you need help in the kitchen?" Honey asks.

"I just put the food out. You can help with the drinks. I have sweet tea," her aunt replies.

The door chimes behind us, and Trent Goldman and his wife Paige enter. After hugs and back-slapping, we sit down at the large table.

"Let's eat while everything's hot. I made chicken and rice," Skipper announces.

The food is already on the table, family style. The aroma of fresh cornbread fills the air, and I slather a hot slice with butter.

Megan leans forward, her eyes sparkling with excitement. "Honey's going to have a baby!"

Skipper gives a pleased nod. "Congratulations!"

I see Trent and Paige glance at each other with a soft smile.

Trent clears his voice and beams. "We're expecting as well. Paige is pregnant."

There is stunned silence for a moment, and then the room erupts in excited chatter.

Paige turns a pretty pink as she and Honey share a hug.

"Our babies will grow up together," Honey says eagerly.

Paige states excitedly, "We can have playdates!"

I walk over to shake Trent's hand. "Congratulations."

Trent is all proud smiles as he returns my handshake. "Same to you, Michael."

TWENTY-EIGHT

After dinner, the girls and Skipper huddle together, their heads bent in animated conversation, their laughter punctuating the air. Trent and I stand to stretch our legs. Matthew gets out an electronic game and settles into a corner.

Trent approaches me and asks, "How's the Mazarano case coming along?"

I state grimly, "We're following every lead we can find." Then I shrug, "But so far, we haven't come up with anything to exonerate our client."

Trent nods solemnly. "Man, that's got to be tough. I'm sure you're under a lot of pressure." He glances at me curiously. "How did you get involved in the case?"

I give a scoffing laugh. "Not by choice." I give him a rueful look. "Believe me, I didn't want to be involved."

Trent nods thoughtfully. "I bet." Then he looks up at me. "Let me know if I can help in any way."

At my surprised look, he states, "I mean. We're related now. Family."

I nod. "Yes, we are." I turn to him and say with a sincere grin. "I appreciate the offer... but I don't want anyone else embroiled in this. Especially family," I say, my eyes filled with meaning.

Trent nods. "Understood."

Trying to lighten the mood. I grin over at him. "Besides, you've got enough on your plate. You're going to be a first-time father." I raise my glass. "To fatherhood."

Trent returns my grin. "I'm scared to death but looking forward to it," he admits.

I laugh. "I was scared, too. I still am, for that matter." My eyes flicker to Megan and Matthew, and I proudly state, "But I wouldn't give up being a father for anything in this world."

A wave of unease surges through me as I think about the Mazarano case and how closely they are watching me and my family. The weight of responsibility feels like a heavy burden on my shoulders. This case can't end soon enough as far as I'm concerned. I want my family and me to be as far away from the mob's influence as possible.

Twenty-Nine

Honey

Michael and I are attending a charity event for MAP, the Mother's Advancement Program. Paige works for the non-profit and invited us to tonight's event.

I glance in the mirror, a bubble of excitement traveling through me. The soft silk of the gown brushes against my skin, sending a shiver of pleasure down my spine. The swirl of colors—peaches and cream with pearl accents on the sleeves—flatters my complexion. The empire waist hides any sign of my baby bump, and the high slit that shows a flash of leg gives it just enough sex appeal.

My long honey-colored hair is swept into an elegant coiffure atop my head, with tendrils framing my face—a pearl-encrusted comb secures it.

My eyeshadow accentuates my eyes, making them look even bigger, and my lipstick gives my smile a glossy peach shine. My pearl earrings and beige high heels complete the look, giving me an air of sophistication. As I twirl in front of the mirror, I can't help but feel a surge of excitement. Tonight is going to be special.

My Aunt Skipper volunteered to have the kids sleep over at her house. Her eyes twinkled as she explained she's practicing for her role as a great-grandmother when she picked them up earlier.

I glance at the clock with a slight frown. Michael should have been home by now.

Right on cue, I hear the front door open and hear his tread on the stairs. I turn toward him with a smile.

Michael comes to an abrupt stop when he sees me. I feel the burn of his gaze as his smoldering eyes rake over me from head to toe.

"You look beautiful," he says in a husky voice.

I feel the blush as it covers my cheeks at his compliment.

"Thank you," I murmur as he approaches me and takes me in his arms.

He murmurs, "You're going to be a temptation all evening."

I laugh as I tilt my head to the side and give him a coy look.

"I thought you barely had time for a shower," I remind him with a teasing smile.

"Dammit! You're right," Michael says as he reluctantly lets me go and strides into the bathroom.

I walk over to the dresser and dab on my favorite perfume. On impulse, with a glance at my plunging neckline, I put a little perfume in the hollow between my breasts, and with a naughty smile, I also place a drop behind each of my knees.

Michael strolls into the bedroom and drops his towel. When he turns, my eyes are drawn to his lean, naked buttocks. I can't drag my eyes away as his muscles bunch. He quickly finishes drying off and then picks up his clothes.

In moments, he's fully dressed and standing in front of the mirror, brushing his dark wavy hair. Michael splashes on some cologne and turns.

"Ready?" he asks, and I nod. "Good, I hired a limousine for the night."

The drive there is filled with anticipation, the Jacksonville city lights blurring past the windows. As we pull up to the hotel, I can't help but feel a surge of excitement.

I look up at the brightly lit hotel. Then the driver opens the car door. Michael slides out and holds out his hand to escort me out of the car and into the building.

I haven't ever attended such a grand event. We make our way to a table in the lobby, and Michael gives our names.

"Mr. and Mrs. Michael Garret." They nod us in.

As we make our entrance, I look around in wonder at the elegantly decorated rooms. The grand ballroom is a glittering spectacle, filled with the sounds of laughter and hushed conversation. Chandeliers, each a cascade of crystal and light, hang from the ornate ceiling, casting a soft, ethereal glow over the crowded room.

The walls are adorned with flowers and gilded mirrors, reflecting the dazzling array of colors and textures. A polished dance floor shimmers under the soft light, inviting couples to twirl and sway to the rhythm of the music.

We look up to see Paige and Trent as they make their way through the crowd to greet us.

"Honey, that's the perfect dress for you," Paige states with a careful hug.

"You look stunning," I compliment her with a smile. I lean forward. "I haven't been to such a sophisticated event before."

Paige smiles in sympathy. "It can be a little overwhelming at first. I used to dread these events when I first started working for my boss, Hunter Henson," she confides. "But now, I look forward to dressing up, and it's for a really great cause."

I nod. "You've told me about the Mother's Advancement Program. It sounds like you're really changing lives for the better."

Paige smiles. "Thank you. I believe in our non-profit." She looks around. "That's my boss over there in the gray suit, and his wife Rebel is in the red dress."

"Hunter will be speaking tonight immediately after dinner, and then there will be dancing." She turns to me with shining eyes. "I promise you'll have fun tonight, and the food is always superb."

Trent and Paige walk through the crowd, introducing us to the people they know. We hear a dinner chime, and Paige explains that we need to find our seats.

"I asked for you and Michael to be seated near us," Paige says easily as she shows us to the correct table.

Michael holds my chair as I sit down. The white tablecloths and shimmering candles give everything an elegant flair.

My eyes linger on Michael's dashing figure in his crisp suit and tie. When he boldly grins back at me, I get a flutter in my stomach. The man is too good-looking, I think breathlessly.

Dinner is a mouth-watering Beef Wellington with grilled asparagus and cheesecake for dessert.

As the dessert is served, Hunter Henson gives a brief presentation on the MAP charity. I listen intently as he explains how the program helps single mothers advance their careers with job placement and assistance. He charmingly asks for donations, and his speech ends with a round of applause from the guests, including me.

We hear the soft strands of music as a band begins to play softly in the background. Michael's vibrant green eyes glimmer with heat.

"Dance with me?" he asks with a sexy smile.

As I slip my hand in his, he pulls me gently to my feet and escorts me to the dance floor. As his broad hands pull me toward him, a shiver of awareness runs down my spine.

The room is flooded with romantic music as we begin to sway. I melt against his harder frame as he wraps his arms tighter around me.

The familiar scent of his cologne beacons me closer, and I relax further against his chest. As the melody soars around us, Michael places a finger under my chin and pulls my face toward his. He brushes his mouth lightly over mine.

When his fingers trace patterns down my back, his touch sets off a spark of awareness that leaves me breathless.

I tilt my head to the side as I feel his lips on my neck. I surrender to the intimate moment. It's like we're surrounded by a bubble—sheltering us from the outside world. I raise my arms and encircle his broad shoulders. His hand brushes my face, then traces my lips with a lingering touch.

I feel my heart begin to pound in my chest, and a rush of longing surges through me. As the soft music washes over us, his hard body brushes intimately against mine, and the crowd completely disappears. I'm lost in the feeling of Michael's strong arms encircling me, keeping me safe.

As the song comes to an end, Michael rubs me against him, and I feel a dampness between my thighs as I ache for him to take me. Claim me. Make me his.

I want more than just his body. I want Michael's heart, but I know that's still out of my reach. So, for now, this is enough. At least that's what I tell my bruised heart. I can feel the need for him as it courses through me like a tidal wave.

"Let's go home," he whispers softly in my ear, and I shiver in response—a slave to my own desires.

Thirty

Michael

As I signal to the driver, he pulls up, and I open the car door for Honey. As she slides in, the slit in her gown gaps, exposing more of her creamy white thigh. My cock forms a bulge in my pants as I instantly harden.

Once the door closes, I roughly pull Honey toward me and claim her lips with a rough kiss. I plunge inside the warm depths of her mouth, stroking her with my tongue as a prequel to what I plan later. I feel her tremble in response and want to rip off her clothes and take her right then, in the back seat of our limo.

As the primal need courses through me, I clench my jaw as I try to reclaim my control. Honey's soft whimper only flames the heat of my desire as I pull her onto my lap. My hand immediately dives between her soft thighs, searching for her moist heat; my only barrier is her silken panties.

I trace a broad finger over the damp fabric covering her core and have to bite back a groan as I feel a surge of wetness. Uncaring of the driver, I push the crotch of her panties out of my way and enter her with a blunt finger. I feel her stiffen in surprise as we're in the back seat of a limo. But as I reach high inside of her, she forgets her surroundings, and I soon have her shuddering in my arms. I glance at the driver, but his eyes wisely remain on the road ahead. He pulls up to the house.

I assist Honey out of the car, helping her stand on shaky legs, and then wave to the driver, glad that I've already taken care of the bill and the tip.

As soon as the front door closes behind us, Honey turns to me. She leans forward and I feel her fingers as she touches my tie. She gives me a sly smile as she loosens it and then uses it to pull me toward her. She leans in and gives me a sultry kiss. Then she steps back with a smile and arches an expectant eyebrow.

I smirk when I see her cheeks are still rosy from my attention to her in the car.

THIRTY

I roughly turn her around, unzip her dress, and let it pool to the floor. Honey is left standing in a peach-colored lace bra. What I thought were panties are actually a thong. My cock feels rock hard at the pictures she makes with her soft skin glowing in her skimpy lingerie.

I shrug out of my jacket and let it fall to the floor. I unbutton my dress shirt, baring my chest, and unfasten my belt.

I grab Honey's hand and head to the closest piece of furniture—the dining room table. Her eyes widen as I pick her up and place her on the polished top. I take the loosened tie from around my neck, and with a smoldering grin, I use it to cover her eyes.

"Just focus on feeling what I do to you," I whisper in her ear, and she nods.

As she leans back against its smooth surface, I spread her legs. I bend her knees and place them over my shoulders. I lean in and give her a long lick, spreading her silky folds. I feel her hips as they lift off the table, but I hold her down with a firm hand on her hip bone.

I then explore her folds as I lick and suck, pushing her thong to the side but not taking it off her.

"You're sweet as honey," I whisper against her thigh.

Her soft moans spur me on. I rear slightly back and slip in a finger. Then two, I'm knuckle deep inside her, and she's losing control as she writhes against me. I continue relentlessly to finger fuck her on the dining room table as her uncontrollable moans fill the air.

"That's it, baby," I say hoarsely. "There's nobody here. You can be as loud as you want."

Honey continues to pant heavily as she nears her climax. I can feel the tremors as they overtake her. She clenches down on my hand. I continue pumping in and out of her until she shatters and cries out.

"Michael!" she screams loudly, and my ears ring as a smug smile creases my face. "Oh, Michael..." Her hands pull tightly on my hair.

Once she's finished, I grin down at her. I slip her legs off my shoulders one at a time, but not before I kiss the backs of her knees.

"You smell good," I whisper against her soft skin.

Honey gives me a weak smile as she's sprawled on the table like a feast before me. I can feel my body start to harden in earnest, waiting greedily for its turn.

THIRTY

I pull Honey's hips toward me, I reach down slip the tie from around her eyes, and toss it aside. Then, as she blinks up at me, her face flushed, I give a wicked smile.

"No, not on the table this time. I want you bent over so I can watch as I take you from behind."

Her eyes widen as I stand her up and walk her toward the couch.

I reach out and arrogantly slip the pearl comb from her hair. My eyes flash in satisfaction as her blonde hair falls about her shoulders.

"Bend over," I demand as I turn her toward the arm of the couch. "That's it. Yes. Looking at you in that thong is making me rock hard. I want to see and feel your lush ass as I take you."

I see how my words increase her passion, and her eyes darken with her arousal. She turns around, and I unhook her bra, letting her full breasts fall forward. I cup her breasts with my hands and fondle her for a few minutes, enjoying the feel of the unbound globes filling my palms.

I can't wait any longer, and I place my hand on her lower back, putting her right where I want her. As she goes to slip off her high heels, I stop her.

"No. Leave them on," I order.

I can hear Honey's harsh breathing as I move closer. I can tell she feels the warmth of my body, but I pause, building the tension and letting her anticipation increase.

Then I slowly unzip my pants, and my eager cock springs free. I move in close behind her and then grasp her hips roughly with my hands. Finally, I spread her folds and enter her in one powerful thrust. Her feet almost lift from the floor from the forceful way I take her.

I wonder for a minute if I'm being too rough, but then Honey arches her back and pushes back and up to meet my strokes. I glance down, wanting to watch as my cock fills her.

I continue to pound into her as a red haze of lust almost blinds me with my primal need. I hear Honey as she starts to pant heavily. The sound of our bodies meeting in rhythm is the only sound in the room as I increase the pace of our lovemaking.

I reach down and press hard on her clit.

I demand, "Now, Honey. Come."

Her body obeys and clenches down on me, milking me in her climax. I shudder as I follow her over the edge and shout my completion. I slump over her back and lightly kiss her neck before I find the strength to stand and help her up.

Her face is flushed, but her eyes glimmer with her satisfaction at our activities.

I reach out and give her a slow kiss.

"See what you do to me?" I ask her in a low voice. Then murmur, "Let's go upstairs to finish."

Honey blinks, and then her eyes widen. She walks over to our discarded clothes, and I laugh as she primly picks them up off the floor. I watch as she looks around, and then I bend over and pick up her lace bra from behind the couch. I let it swing from my fingers as I hold it out to her with an arrogant smile.

She grins as she takes the slip of lace from my hand. I take some of the clothes from her, and we head up the stairs and into our bedroom.

"It's going to be a long night," I promise her with a heated gaze.

The next morning, I blink from the glare of the sun as it streams through our bedroom window, feeling Honey stir beside me.

Without opening my eyes, I ask. "When is your aunt bringing the kids home?"

"Not until noon," I hear her soft reply.

I grin. "What time is it now?"

"Nine o'clock," she answers, as I feel her twist toward the clock.

I open my eyes and roll on top of her. "That's enough time," I murmur as I spread her legs.

It's almost noon when we finally exit our bedroom, fully dressed. We would have been ready sooner if we didn't have to stop every few minutes and kiss each other. Honey was irresistible, and I couldn't keep my hands from reaching out to caress her lush ass or cup a soft breast.

Even now, she's like a drug, and I feel addicted to her honey-like sweetness.

When the doorbell rings, I reluctantly loosen my hold on her. Honey's eyes are bright when she opens the door for her aunt and the children.

A surge of disappointment goes through me that our intimate time alone has come to an end. I love my children, but I've greatly enjoyed my evening alone with Honey.

THIRTY

Her Aunt Skipper surveys us both with a shrewd smile.

"Humph. I remember what it's like to be married with kids," she says, throwing us a knowing smile. "If you need me to watch the children again, just let me know."

She then turns and gives Megan and Matthew a fond smile.

"It was fun. Maybe next time, we'll go to MOSH or the zoo," she states with a smile.

Megan and Matthew both nod.

"Cool," Matthew says as he loves the zoo and the Museum of Science and History.

Megan grins. "Sure! Skipper, that sounds great." She turns to us. "Can we, Dad?"

I nod. "Of course."

The kids hug Skipper goodbye and then bound up the stairs to their rooms.

I give Skipper an appreciative smile. "Thanks again. Honey and I appreciate the offer."

Skipper walks over to the dining room table, bends over, and picks up my tie. She hands it to a blushing Honey with a smirk and a twinkle in her eye.

"Yes, I'm sure you do," she says drily. With a wink, Skipper leaves, closing the front door behind her.

Thirty-One

Honey

Michael and I are attending our first PTA parent-teacher conference tonight. The schools are hosting them on the same night. First up is Matthew's school, then we'll go to Megan's.

As we enter the hallway, Michael turns to me.

"What is it about visiting a school? It always takes me back to when I was a child. I remember walking the halls and even how it felt to be sent to the principal's office." He grimaces. "No matter how old I get, a school still takes me back to the past."

With a playful glint in my eye, I say, "I feel the same way." Then I admit in a flippant tone, "Except I was never sent to the principal's office."

Michael nods his head. "Yeah, I can see that. You were one of those goody two-shoes girls that sucked up to the teachers."

"I was not!" I say with pretend outrage. "And nobody says goody two shoes anymore."

"Yet, you know what it means," he says deadpan. "Yep, you were one of those goody-goody girls who never did anything wrong."

"And it sounds like you were one of those boys that were constantly in trouble for picking on us." I tilt my chin with a lofty air.

Michael reaches out, takes my hand, and murmurs, "When all we really wanted was to get you girls to notice us."

I give him a wide smile, but the classroom door behind us opens before I can respond.

"Mr. and Mrs. Garret? Please come in. I'm Sarah Miller, Matthew's teacher." She gives us a friendly smile. "Nice to meet you both."

She waves us in and shows us to our seats.

THIRTY-ONE

"Matthew is doing well in his classes. He struggles a bit with math but is still progressing."

Michael and I listen attentively as the teacher goes over Matthew's strengths. All in all, I feel very proud of the feedback she gives us on Matthew. I glance over at Michael, and he's beaming with the same pride that I feel. He reaches over and squeezes my hand with a grin.

The teacher looks up and states warmly, "Matthew mentioned last week that he's going to have a little brother or sister."

Michael smiles over at me. "Yes, my wife is expecting."

"I'm happy for you both," Matthew's teacher states with a smile.

We ask a few more questions, then stand and shake her hand when our allotted time is up. Michael thanks her for the great job she's doing.

As we turn to leave, we see Lisa and John Johnson entering the room. Sarah, Matthew's teacher, nods at them and turns to us.

"Goodbye, Mr. and Mrs. Garret. Congratulations again on the baby."

At her words, Lisa's husband, John, gets a knowing look on his face as he looks from us to his wife.

"I knew you guys had something going on the night Matthew broke his arm," he says slyly as he slaps Michael on the back.

I watch as Michael clenches his jaw. "Lisa, John." He gives them a curt nod.

Michael takes my hand and grimly pulls me into the hallway.

Lisa gives us an embarrassed look at her husband's comment but otherwise doesn't say anything. I feel almost sorry for her, having a man like John for her husband. I can't imagine what it must be like to be married to someone so disrespectful and insensitive.

We walk silently through the mostly empty halls. The only sound is the click of our shoes echoing down the hallway and the occasional low hum of a conversation or two with a teacher or parent as we pass a classroom. Gone is the playful banter we shared earlier. I give a tentative glance at Michael. His face is tight, and he's still scowling.

I gently squeeze his hand, and his eyebrows raise in surprise.

"Michael, don't let John's snide comments get to you," I say in a low voice.

THIRTY-ONE

His frown deepens. "I didn't like his insinuations." He then confesses, "I didn't like the way he looked at you. He tried to cheapen what we have."

"Well, I, for one, don't care what someone like John Johnson thinks. Lisa is nice, but he's not anyone I would ever consider as a friend."

Michael turns and gives me a searching look.

Then he gives me a small smile. "You really didn't take offense at what he said?"

I shrug. "I've never liked the guy. While I don't like his comments, I don't pay him any attention, and I doubt other parents will either."

Michael only nods at my words, but I notice that the tension has left his shoulders.

I raise my eyebrow and state dryly, "Besides. I notice he thought it was great that you knocked up the nanny."

I hear Michael chuckle as he corrects me, "A younger, beautiful nanny."

Now it's my turn to laugh.

It's the weekend, and Matthew has his first youth track and field meet. He practically bounced up and down on the car ride over. We leave him with his team and coach and take our seats in the bleachers.

I gratefully adjust the baseball cap Michael gave me as it shields my eyes from the sun's glaring rays. It's hot, but an occasional breeze offers a welcome respite.

Michael whistled when I came out wearing navy blue shorts and a halter top that accentuates my curves, leaving my shoulders bare. He makes a striking figure himself in shorts and a T-shirt that calls attention to his chiseled chest and muscular biceps.

Michael suddenly stands and throws me a grin.

"Why don't I get all of us something to drink?" he says.

"I'll go with you. It's hot just sitting here," Megan declares as she makes a face.

I watch as they disappear up the bleachers. I glance up a few minutes later to see a stranger with his hands full. The man takes a seat on the bench in front of me.

My eyes search the field, hoping for a glimpse of Matthew, but I don't see him yet.

"Hey, I haven't seen you here before," the guy comments with a friendly grin.

"This is my first time here," I respond with a polite smile.

"At least you dressed appropriately," he says easily. "The sun's brutal today."

"Yes, it is," I agree with a nod.

The guy suddenly turns his entire body around so he can face me.

"So, what's your name—"

"Honey Garret," I hear Michael say as his possessive gaze lands on me. "And I'm Michael Garret, her husband."

The guy blinks as he takes in Michael's possessive stance. Megan stands behind her father, holding her beverage. As they settle into the empty seats beside me, the guy gives us an awkward smile. He then gathers up his drink and hotdog and stands.

"My friends have arrived," he murmurs to no one in particular and hurriedly walks away.

Michael turns to me. "Was that guy hitting on you?" He says with a scowl.

"I don't know," I shrug. "I thought he was just being friendly."

Michael frowns, and we both follow the guy as he picks a bench by another single lady.

"He was hitting on you," he states firmly.

I raise my eyebrow and state, "Whether he was or wasn't, your caveman vibe scared him away."

"Caveman, huh?" Michael snickers.

Megan chimes in. "Yeah, Dad, you didn't look very friendly."

"Good." Michael hands me my drink and settles into his seat with a satisfied smirk.

A wave of hope surges through me as I bask in Michael's possessiveness. I give an inward smile.

We eagerly lean forward when it's Matthew's turn on the track. We cheer him on loudly and clap when he comes in second for his age group.

We head toward the parking lot when the meet is over and the bleachers empty. We spy Matthew, his face flushed with excitement as he talks to his coach. His coach leans forward and then nods to us. Matthew smiles up at him, turns, and races madly toward us, his fists in the air.

"Dad! Mom! Did you see me?" he yells as he approaches. "Did you see? I came in second place!"

My heart pounds loudly in my chest, and I give Matthew a watery smile as I fight to hide my emotional response to being called mom. Michael's arm goes around me as he pulls me securely to his side. His warm eyes find mine over Matthew's head, and I give him a trembling smile.

Michael gives Matthew a proud grin. "You did a great job, son. Second place is wonderful."

Even Megan gives him a side hug and states, "Nice job!"

I finally find my voice and say huskily, "Matt, you ran like the wind."

Matthew is practically bursting with pride at our praise as he clambers into the car.

Michael glances into the back seat and says, "I think this calls for an ice cream celebration!"

Michael then glances at me and says softly, "What do you think, Mom?"

I blink back my emotional tears and nod around the lump in my throat.

Thirty-Two

Michael

It's been a rough morning. My team and I are leaving no stone unturned on the Mazarano case. Another status report is due, but we haven't uncovered any new information.

I run my hand wearily through my hair, a knot tightening in my stomach. Vito Mazarano is not a patient man.

I look up as a soft knock on my office door pulls me from my thoughts.

A slow smile spreads across my face when I see Honey standing there.

THIRTY-TWO

"This is a nice surprise. Come in," I say, standing and walking around my desk to greet her with a quick kiss.

Honey smiles and glances around my office. "I've only been here once before when you asked me to drop something off."

I nod. "I remember," I take her hand. "Why don't I show you around the place?"

I give her a brief tour, introducing her to a few colleagues we meet along the way.

"I need to check my emails. Then, maybe we could grab some lunch?" I suggest. Her eyes light up with a smile as she nods.

When I escort her back to my office, Nancy, my administrative assistant, returns from an early lunch.

"Nancy, you remember Honey, don't you?" I introduce them.

Nancy smiles. "Of course. It's Mrs. Garret now." She gives Honey a swift hug.

"I just need to check something, and then I'll be leaving for lunch," I inform my admin.

Honey follows me into my office and stands at the tall glass windows, looking out at the city view while I check my laptop. As I close the lid, I glance up, and Honey's hair shimmers in the sunlight that streams in from the plate glass window. She looks like a vision as it casts her in a warm glow. The feminine sundress she is wearing shows off her curvy figure.

I walk over to her and wrap my arms around her. The heat of her skin sends awareness shooting through me. We stand looking out at the cityscape as I slowly rub my hands up and down her arms.

Honey's breath catches as I lean in. A wisp of her intoxicating floral perfume envelopes me. It feels like a silent invitation as my lips graze the tender skin of her neck. She shivers softly in my arms as her eyes flutter shut.

A blush slowly creeps up her neck, painting her cheeks a pretty pink. The outside world fades away as I press my lips to hers. I savor her honeyed taste before deepening the kiss, her lips parting under mine.

As she melts against me, the outside world dims around us, and my desire builds.

A sharp rap on the door startles us apart, shattering the intimate moment.

I feel irritation surge through me as Vito's goons, Marcel and Bruno, push into my office as if they own the place.

THIRTY-TWO

I loosen my hold on Honey but keep her close to me as I turn.

"Gentlemen," I say in a flat voice.

"Garret, it appears you're busy," Marcel says slyly, "Unfortunately, Mr. Mazarano wanted us to remind you that he's eager for your status report."

I nod. "I sent it a few minutes ago. He can call me if he has any questions."

They exchange a knowing look and snicker. "Vito Mazarano doesn't make phone calls. He sends us."

I narrow my eyes at them as Marcel's beady black eyes rove over Honey's form. I deliberately step in front of her, blocking his view.

"Please tell your boss that following leads takes time," I say quietly. "As soon as we have something new, we'll notify him."

Marcel studies me for a moment. "I'll give him the message." As he and Bruno reach the door, he turns back. "Time is running out, Garret." His eyes are cold, devoid of warmth.

I give him a curt nod. "I'm aware," I fire back.

"Garret," he gives a thin smile. "Mrs. Garret."

The door clicks shut behind them, and Honey shivers. I turn toward her and her eyes are wide with concern.

"Michael? Those men work for Vito Mazarano? Your client's father?" She asks with a frown tinged with worry. "Isn't he part of the mob?"

I let out a silent laugh. "Part of the mob? No, he's the leader of the mob," I correct her.

Honey silently searches my face. "This is why you said the timing was bad. You're worried about what will happen if you lose your case, aren't you?"

"Yes," I admit my voice rough. "I'm worried what Vito Mazarano will do to you and the kids."

Honey wraps her arms around me in a hug. She leans back slightly, cupping my face with her hands.

"Michael, I believe in you."

The simple trust reflected in her brown eyes brings me to my knees. It breaks me and fills me with strength all at the same time.

"Thank you, Honey," I say, a mix of emotions unfurling in my chest at her unwavering faith. "I'll try not to let you down."

THIRTY-TWO

I clear my throat. "Where would you like to go for lunch?"

"Surprise me," she says softly, taking my hand.

We walk into the Olive Tree, a quaint Mediterranean restaurant on Hendricks Avenue. Honey bites her lip as she peruses their menu.

She finally turns toward me and asks, "What are you having?"

I smile. "The fish tacos are my favorite. Their falafel with hummus and pita bread is good also."

We place our orders and sit down across from each other in a booth. The lively music playing through the speakers drowns out the other diners, and the smell of sizzling spicy food mixes in the air making our mouths water.

When our food is placed in front of us, I watch as Honey takes a tentative bite. She then smiles up at me, her eyes shining her approval.

"This is delicious! I see why you chose this place," she says with a satisfied smile.

My gaze becomes heated as I watch her daintily lick a bit of sauce from her fingers. I shift restlessly in my seat, dragging my eyes away.

Our lunch conversation is light and general. I can tell that Honey is trying to take my mind off Vito's goon's unexpected visit. So, I listen intently as she updates me on a few things she picked out for the nursery.

"Paige and I decided to have a joint baby shower," she tells me. "Closer to our due dates."

"A joint baby shower?" I say in a doubt-filled voice. "How would that work?"

"Well, it's basically two showers. We'd share the cake, but we wouldn't share the presents," she says with a twinkle in her eyes. "We thought it would be easier for my sisters and Aunt Skip."

"My dad and grandpa will probably come with them." She continues with a sideways glance. "If they do, would you be able to spend time with them during the baby shower?"

"Sure," I say easily. "It'll give us a chance to get to know each other better."

Honey gives me a grateful smile. "Thanks, Michael." She covers my hand with hers.

After I walk Honey to her car, we share another slow kiss.

THIRTY-TWO

"Drop by anytime you want to, Honey," I reassure as I open her car door.

I stand there, lost in thought, a soft smile on my face as she drives away.

Back in my office, Trent Goldman arrives and strides in with a nod.

"Trent! What brings you by?" I ask curiously.

"I know a guy with the FBI," he says cautiously. "They don't give out information. So, you can't mention how you learned about this. Okay?"

I nod and lean forward with interest. "Understood."

"An acquaintance let it slip that Zappo was going to be testifying in court. He was going to enter their witness protection program. Before he was killed," he says grimly.

I frown and cross my arms suspiciously. "You and I both know that the FBI doesn't let anything just slip. Especially about something as confidential as witness protection. Even if the guy is dead."

Trent grimaces. "I agree. I felt it was deliberate."

I rub my chin. "Did they tell you who he was testifying against? Was it Victor or Vito Mazarano?" I ask sharply.

"No. He only mentioned that their lead witness was a no-go since Zappo turned up dead." Trent furrows his brows. "It's a possible lead, but you'll have to confirm if it's legit or not," Trent says warily.

"Thanks, Trent. My team and I will get right on this."

Trent nods and turns toward the door. Then he stops and glances back.

"Watch your back, Michael. This could be a trap," he says in a cautious tone. "I'm always suspicious of this type of information."

"I feel the same," I say grimly. "I'll be careful."

Thirty-Three

Honey

Michael again accompanies me to my ultrasound. This time, we're both excited because we should be able to find out if we're having a boy or a girl. Michael's been wonderful to me as my baby hormones have turned me into one big jumble of emotions. The other night, he caught me crying during a TV commercial that showed a quivering puppy.

He didn't laugh or roll his eyes like I half-expected. Instead, he pulled me close, his arms warm and steady as the tears soaked through his shirt. I know I'm a mess—having to pee every ten minutes, forbidden from lifting anything heavier than a milk jug—but somehow, Michael makes it easier.

I smile to myself, remembering how Matthew keeps calling me "Mom." Every time he says it, my heart skips a beat, like I'm hearing it for the first time. Megan still calls me Honey, and that's okay. She was older when Michelle passed.

Michael is tapping on his phone while we wait for the ultrasound technician to arrive, but I can feel the current of excitement simmering beneath his calm exterior. His eyes glance over to me every few seconds, and I can tell he's just as impatient as I am. The doctor spoke to us earlier, but it was brief. She promised to go over everything with us once she had the results.

The door slides open, and the same ultrasound technician from last time enters, her familiar smile warm and reassuring. Michael slips his phone into his pocket, and just as she glides the wand across my round belly, the swishing sound of our baby's heartbeat fills the room. I freeze, my breath catching.

Michael gently squeezes my hand, his grip solid and comforting as my eyes widen, the wonder of the moment washing over me. I glance at the screen, trying to make sense of the blurry gray swirls. But nothing I see resembles a baby in my mind, but I feel the anticipation building inside me...

The technician pauses and gives us a soft smile. "Would you like to know the sex of your baby?"

Michael and I look at her with anticipation shining in our eyes. We both nod, not trusting ourselves to speak.

"It's a girl."

I feel my smile widen, and I immediately glance up at Michael. He beams down at me, his eyes sparkling.

"A girl," he whispers, leaning in to place a gentle kiss on my forehead. "That's perfect. Sugar and spice and everything nice."

After the tech leaves, I place my hand lovingly over my abdomen. A soft smile still on my lips. A little girl! My heart swells with so much love for the tiny being growing inside me that I can hardly breathe.

Michael places his broad hand over mine, and it's warm and steady. I look up at him, my eyes brimming with tears. I try to swallow past the lump in my throat.

"Hey, you doing okay?" Michael asks, his voice barely over a whisper, his eyes filled with tenderness.

At my teary nod and watery smile, he grins. "It's a bit overwhelming, isn't it? The emotions?"

I sniff and nod. He reaches out and gathers me gently into an embrace. He simply holds me. And for a moment, that's enough—just him, me, and our baby girl.

A few minutes later, the doctor strides in with a cheerful smile.

"A little girl! Congratulations." She smiles. "Everything appears normal. Your blood pressure's good, baby's healthy." She glances at me. "How are you feeling?"

I give her a sheepish smile. "I'm so emotional all the time. I cry at the silliest things," I admit, wiping at my damp cheeks. "And I'm craving spicy foods and ice cream... at the same time."

The doctor laughs. "Both of those are pretty common." She turns toward Michael. "I had a patient once who craved Taco Bell at two in the morning."

Michael chuckles. "Hasn't come to that yet."

"As long as the cravings aren't harmful and you watch the spice level, you should be fine," the doctor says with a reassuring smile.

Once we're back in the car, Michael turns to me, eyes bright.

"I'm taking a break from the office. Would you like to go shopping for the nursery?"

THIRTY-THREE

"Absolutely," I answer with a bright smile.

We spend the rest of the day picking out furniture and decorations for the baby's room, excitedly planning every little detail. The furniture won't be delivered for a few weeks, but we picked out the perfect wallpaper mural for the main wall—a forest of baby animals. The rest of the room will be painted a soft, pale yellow. Everything is coming together.

When we arrive home, Michael carries the packages upstairs, placing them in the nursery closet until the room is painted and ready. As I stand in the doorway, watching him work, I can't help but feel the quiet joy bubbling up inside me again.

A little girl. Part Michael and part me... Our little girl.

After the front door closes behind Michael, I drift back up to the nursery. I stand in the center of the room, slowly turning in a circle, trying to imagine what the finished space will look like.

Something flutters down off the closet shelf—a soft whisper in the quiet room. I glance down and see that it's an envelope, yellowed at the edges from age. I slowly walk over and pick it up. It's addressed to Michelle Garret, and my heart skips a beat. The slanted handwriting across the front—It's Michael's.

My hand trembles as I hold the envelope, uncertainly creeping in. I glance up and see a small cardboard box tipped on its side. I reach up until my fingers brush the edge and carefully pull it down, trying not to spill any more of the contents.

The box is filled with letters. Love letters. From Michael to Michelle.

A throbbing ache starts in my chest. I slowly sit down on the rocking chair, the small box on my lap, the envelope clutched in my hand. I feel torn between my curiosity and respecting Michael's privacy.

Finally, my curiosity wins out, and I pull out the letter with trembling hands and slowly read it.

> *Michelle,*
> *My love. I miss you. It's only been a few days, but you're constantly in my thoughts.*
> *When the conference speaker is talking, I only hear you, how you giggle uncontrollably sometimes at a joke. I see your sparkling eyes and all the other little things you do.*
> *I am so in love with you.*
> *I especially miss making love to you. But that's only part of it.*
> *I also miss your smile and laughter.*

THIRTY-THREE

> *I can't imagine my life without you in it.*
> *I will only ever love you, Michelle.*
> *No other woman will do. Only you. My love, my wife, my life.*
> *Yours forever,*
> *Michael*

The words slice through me, sharp as a blade, right to my heart. I clutch my chest, gasping as the pain spreads. Hot tears slip down my cheeks. I rock back and forth in the chair, desperate for the ache to subside, but it lingers, deep and relentless.

I'm such a fool to think that Michael could ever love me! I blankly re-read the letter, like probing a sore tooth and a fresh set of hot tears spill over.

I don't know how long I sit there before a numbness settles in, dulling the edges of the pain. But the hurt remains, simmering beneath the surface.

I silently fold the letter, my movements slow, robotic. I place it back in the box with the others. My fingers trail over the cardboard edges, the weight of it heavy in my lap.

I wearily stand. When I place the box back on the shelf, my arms feel weak shaky with my emotions. I push it to the very back of the closet, hidden, out of sight.

I walk to our bedroom, my feet heavy with the weight of what I've just read. In the bathroom, I face the mirror. The woman staring back at me looks like a stranger—her eyes glassy, her skin blotchy and red—a ghost of who she was before.

I blindly reach for a towel, my gaze still locked on my reflection. I see the raw pain reflected in my dark eyes. Shadows that weren't there before. I suddenly bring the towel to my face and sob into it. My heart feels like it's breaking.

When I eventually look up again, my eyes are swollen and puffy. I look even worse. I bend and splash cold water on my face, welcoming the sting as it pulls me away from my downward-spiraling thoughts.

Letters... love letters. They must have been Michelle's thing. Her letter to me after the wedding made me feel hope, but this letter crushes any hope I had left.

I suddenly lift my chin, and I watch my eyes harden in the mirror. Michael wasn't in love with me when we married. I knew that. I knew what I was getting into. So, why does reading his letter hurt so much? What's really changed?

Nothing. Not really. I just found some old romantic letters... and reading about his love... hurt.

But I made my choice. I married him, knowing he could never love me like he loved her. I convinced myself that my love for him could be enough.

My eyes fall on my baby bump—round and full beneath my hand. Our baby girl. I'm going to be a mother. I have a good life. Michael is a good man, a good father, and husband. I will never want for anything... except his love.

I wince as my inner voice whispers the truth to me, and I take a gulping breath.

I need to think of the baby. This rollercoaster of emotions can't be good for her. I rub my stomach, the familiar motion soothing as I let out a shaky sigh.

I can either let this tear me apart, or I can accept the life I have—one that's full of blessings, even without the kind of love I've always longed for.

So, which do I choose? Misery... or to be content with what I have?

Thirty-Four

Michael

The next week is a whirlwind. My team and I scrutinize every detail, combing through mountains of paperwork in preparation for the looming court date. Every word, every piece of evidence—it all has to be airtight.

I shove the file away, the words blurring before me. Exhaustion weighs on me as I lean back in my chair, staring blankly out the windows at the city skyline. But I don't really see it. Instead, my mind goes back to this morning, back to Honey.

Lately, there's been a sadness in her eyes—a quiet longing. I don't like how it makes me feel. When I catch her haunted gaze, I want to hold her and chase all the shadows away. But

THIRTY-FOUR

I made a promise to myself. I can't let her mean too much to me.

Losing Michelle to cancer was devastating. It nearly destroyed me, and I swore I'd never go through that kind of pain again. I don't think I could survive it a second time. I thought I could care for her without letting her get too close.

But Honey... she's different. She's already slipping through the cracks in my armor, finding her way into my heart despite my best efforts to keep her at arm's length. And it's getting harder to push her away.

My phone buzzes on the desk, pulling me back to reality.

"Michael, your team's waiting for you in the conference room," Nancy, my admin, informs me.

"Thanks, Nancy." I hang up, taking a deep breath before heading to join my team.

The room is filled with muted conversations and shuffling papers when I enter.

"Anything new to report?" I ask, scanning the faces around the table.

One of the newer members, eager to make a good impression, speaks up. He's pouring over the coroner's report of the murder victim, Frank Zappo.

"I have the details of the report. The victim had ID on him, but his girlfriend had to identify the body since his face was... well, unrecognizable." The rookie looks up, wincing. "Looks like he was beaten pretty badly. Hope that happened after he was dead."

He goes back to the report. "The stomach contents were shrimp and crab... at least he had a good last meal," he says jokingly, trying to lighten the mood, but his joke falls flat.

I stiffen, my eyes narrowing at him. "What was that last part?" I ask, my tone sharper than intended.

The young man grimaces. "Sorry, Michael. I didn't mean to disrespect the dead—"

"Not that," I cut him off, waving it away. "The last line. Read it again."

"Uh, right," he stammers. "Stomach contents contained recently eaten shrimp and crab proteins."

I step closer, scanning the report myself. My mind races as I read the line over again.

THIRTY-FOUR

"When I represented Frank Zappo five years ago, we met at a seafood restaurant. I remember him clearly saying he was allergic to shellfish."

I look around the room, my pulse quickening.

"We need to get Frank's medical records. A statement from his doctor—anything that can confirm his allergy."

The energy in the room shifts as my team picks up on the significance. Eyes brighten, pens scratch across paper, and the mood becomes energized by this unexpected lead.

"If Frank was allergic to shellfish, then we have two possibilities. Either the deceased isn't Frank Zappo, or someone tried to poison him before finishing the job."

I look around the room, my voice grim. "Somebody get the girlfriend down here. Now."

Within the hour, Connie Monty steps into the room. I study her as she sits down. Tight dress, heels, heavy makeup that doesn't quite mask the signs of aging. Her long nails are painted a bright, shiny red. She looks nervous.

"Ms. Monty. Please, have a seat," I greet her, my tone neutral. It's just me, her, and two of my senior team members in the small room.

She sits, eyeing me warily. "I was told you needed to ask me some questions. I've already talked to the police—"

"Yes, we've gone over your deposition," I say with a polite smile. "I knew Frank. I represented him about five years ago."

Connie's lips curl into a brief smile. "Frank mentioned you. Said you were good at what you do."

"Is that all he said?" I ask, watching her closely.

She hesitates, then adds, "He warned me you were like a dog with a bone."

I chuckle softly. "I'm sure he meant that in the best way possible."

Connie narrows her eyes but says nothing.

"I'll get right to the point." I watch her closely. "You identified the body?"

She licks her lips. "That's right."

"How did you know it was Frank?" I ask.

"It was his body," she replies with a nonchalant shrug.

"You were sure it was him?" I press, studying her reaction.

THIRTY-FOUR

"Yes." Connie's voice takes on a coy edge. "You don't spend four years with someone and not recognize their body."

I nod, beginning to pace. Connie fidgets, her discomfort obvious.

"Ms. Monty—"

"Call me Connie," she offers, trying to regain control.

"Alright, Connie," I say, pausing. "Were you aware that Frank was allergic to shellfish?"

She blinks, clearly caught off guard. "Yes, he had one of those pens... for emergencies."

"An epi-pen?" I clarify.

"Yeah, that's it. He always carried it with him," she says, crossing her legs confidently.

I lean in slightly. "Were you aware that the body you identified had shrimp and crab in the stomach?"

Her face turns pale, and a sheen of sweat breaks out on her upper lip. She avoids my eyes, licking her lips nervously.

"No, I was never told that..." her voice trails off weakly, and her eyes remain downcast.

"Connie," I say, voice low and steady, "is Frank Zappo alive?"

Her face drains of all color. Her hands tremble in her lap, and she shifts uncomfortably.

"How would I know?" she stammers, sounding defensive.

I nod. Noticing Connie didn't say no. My look is direct, and I don't let up.

I lean forward. "I've discovered that Frank was about to enter the witness protection program. Who was he going to testify against?"

Her eyes widen in panic, darting desperately around the room, looking for an escape route.

"Connie," I say in a softer tone. "Victor Mazarano faces jail time for murder. His father, Vito Mazarano, will never let that happen. I can help protect Frank—from the Mazarano family and anyone else who might want him dead."

I watch as she clutches her hands together in her lap, knuckles white. She gives me an uncertain look.

"The Mazarano family isn't the only game in town," she says pointedly.

THIRTY-FOUR

"Okay, but then who was Frank going to testify against?" I press again, more sternly this time.

"I need to go," she suddenly blurts out, rising from her chair. "If I can... I'll pass on this information," she stammers.

I nod and hand her my card. "Tell Frank that time is running out. It's just a matter of time before others discover this."

I glance at the two senior members when the door closes behind her.

"Frank Zappo is alive," I state flatly.

The two young men grin, but I continue to frown.

One of them states with a confused look, "That's good news then. Right, Michael?"

I don't share his enthusiasm. "If the Mazarano family discovers this, they won't just kill Frank. They'll make it public to clear Victor's name."

Both men exchange glances, their faces growing serious as they grasp the implications.

"We need to bring Frank in and get him into the witness protection plan, pronto. At least that way, he'll be alive. This may be the only option that doesn't involve a body bag," I say, my jaw tight.

I pull out my phone and dial a number.

"Trent, I need you to contact your FBI connection. Tell him Frank Zappo may be alive and still able to testify. I need him to call me ASAP. Trent, don't mention this to anyone else. Understood?"

I hang up and look at the two senior members solemnly.

"Gentlemen, I don't think I need to say this, but I will. Everything you've heard is confidential. If the Mazarano family gets wind of this, Frank's as good as dead. Our silence is crucial."

They nod, their expressions somber, understanding what is at stake.

Thirty-Five

Honey

I called Aunt Skipper earlier, and she was more than happy to pick up the kids for the night. I've planned a romantic dinner out for Michael and me—a small surprise to break up the long, grueling hours he's been putting in at work.

Lately, the weight of his stress has started to show. It's etched into the lines of his face, deepening each day. I can see it in the way his shoulders sag when he walks through the door and the absentminded way he eats dinner without really tasting it.

Tonight, I want to take that away, even if just for a little while.

I look around the house, making sure everything's set. Candles, check. Sparkling grape juice chilling, check. My dress, a soft blush that I know he loves, hangs ready in the bedroom. I've even got his favorite music softly playing in the background for when we return home.

I hope tonight reminds him of us—of the connection we used to share when I was just his nanny and the kids went to bed... before the world, and this case demanded so much from him.

As the clock hands get closer to five, I go upstairs, shower, and change into my dress. I leave my makeup light, with just a touch of mascara and a shimmering lip gloss. I slip on my high heels and go downstairs to wait.

When Michael comes through the door, he looks around in surprise.

"Where's the kids?" he asks, his eyes widening as they fall on me.

"They're with Aunt Skipper for the night," I say with a soft smile. "I thought we deserved a date night."

"You want to go out?" he asks.

I suddenly hesitate as I spot the weariness in his eyes.

"We don't have to. Why don't you just relax on the couch?"

He gives me a grateful smile and throws his jacket over a chair. I watch as he settles into the couch, his head resting back on the cushions.

Even with the stress etched on his face, his masculine jaw and dark good looks steal my breath away. I slowly approach him, wanting nothing more than to ease his tension and take his mind off his troubles.

His eyes open and then widen as I kneel in front of him. I slyly move between his legs, and he shifts them even wider. I reach out with a wicked grin. The sound of me lowering his zipper can be heard over the soft strands of music and his sudden intake of breath.

I reach in and boldly cup his manhood, and he softly groans as I stroke him from root to tip. I hear his breathing increase as I lean down and lick the tip of him, pushing my tongue into the slot at the top. I glance up at him with a heated gaze and see his intense green eyes watching my every move. I lean forward and take him into my mouth. I continue to lick and suck him as I caress this silky hard length.

My palm cups his ball sack while I pay special attention to the sensitive underside skin. Then I again take him into my wet mouth.

I feel his hands go into my hair, urging me on as he begins stroking into my mouth.

"Honey, I love seeing your pink lips around my cock," he mutters in a guttural voice. "Oh, baby, that's hot."

I don't hesitate and continue working him with my mouth. A minute or two later.

"Honey, I'm... close. Did you hear me?" his voice hoarse, his hands tightening in my hair.

I suddenly deep-throat him and hear him groan as he hits the back of my throat. I don't stop, at least not until he shouts and then orgasms hard. When I finally lean back and glance up at him, I see that he's wearing a slight smile.

"Damn. You're so good at that," he murmurs appreciatively as he pulls me up and into his arms.

"Thanks," I murmur softly. I feel a wave of satisfaction when I look at his face and see the stress lines are gone, replaced with another type of emotion, as he continues to smile.

He tugs me closer and says with a sigh, "It's good to be home."

I give him a sweet smile. He glances at me and gives a soft chuckle. "Honey, how can you look so sweet and innocent when, only a moment ago, you were such a sexy siren? Doing such naughty things with your pretty little mouth." He brushes his lips across my cheek as he pulls me closer.

His eyes then fall on my dress and he says, "Why don't I order dinner, and we can both get comfortable?"

I arch an eyebrow. "Make that spicy Mexican, and you've got a deal."

Michael changes into jogging pants and a T-shirt, and I slip on sleep shorts and a cami.

When the food arrives, we sit around the dining room table, laughing and talking quietly about everything under the sun. We discuss names for our baby girl.

The warm look in Michael's eyes and the gentle way he touches me almost makes me forget that he isn't in love with me, that his heart will always belong to another. Someone I can't even feel jealous of because she's long gone—forever in the past.

At least I can give him this: sexual satisfaction, my undying love, and a warm haven to come home to.

I suddenly feel the need to confess my love, not in the heat of passion.

Now, while the love I feel for him feels so strong that I can't contain the words.

"Honey? Are you okay, sweetheart?" He asks with a concerned look on his face.

"Yes. I'm fine," I assure him. I look deeply into his eyes. "I love you, Michael."

He falls silent. Reaching out, he gently takes my hand. "I know. You're a very loving woman."

Michael hesitates as if he wants to say more and then looks down at our hands.

He stammers, "I... I care for you, Honey—"

I lean forward. "I don't expect you to say it back, Michael. I just needed to tell you," my voice barely above a whisper.

I watch as his concerned eyes search mine. I don't try to hide the love that's shining out of them. Freely given. He suddenly swallows, and his face clears as he sees the truth of my words in my eyes.

"Thank you, Honey," he says hoarsely. "I don't deserve your love... and I don't deserve you—but you enrich my life in so many ways... and I'm selfish enough to take whatever you're willing to give."

He takes my hand and raises it to his lips for a kiss. "You deserve more than I can offer you," he says, and I can see the deep regret in his green eyes.

"We don't choose who we love, Michael," I tell him with a soft smile.

Later in bed, he pulls me gently toward him and holds me as I fall asleep.

Saturday morning, comes softly, as the house is quiet with the children at my aunt's. The silence without Saturday cartoons seems unnatural.

I reach out, but Michael's side of the bed is empty. The sheets are cold. He's been up for a while.

The door opens, and a rumpled Michael stands there with a lopsided grin and a tray in his hands.

"I made us breakfast," he murmurs with a sleepy smile. "Nothing fancy," he says as he places the tray over my knees.

I look down to see a few Everything bagels smothered in cream cheese, two glasses of orange juice, and a mug of hot coffee.

"The coffee's mine," Michael says as he picks it up and takes a swig.

After we finish breakfast, we snuggle back against the pillows and discuss our plans for the day.

"Aunt Skip said she'd bring the children home around noon," I tell Michael.

"Uh-huh," he mumbles. He rolls close and bares my rounded belly.

"Hey there, baby girl. I'm your daddy. Your mommy and I can't wait to meet you," he says softly, his lips against my skin.

I look down at him, not even trying to hide the love glistening in my eyes. He glances up and grins. He leans back down and playfully blows a loud raspberry on my belly. It tickles, and I giggle uncontrollably.

"Michael!" I gasp in between my laughter. "Stop, Stop! That tickles."

He stops the raspberries but continues whispering loving words to our tiny daughter. I watch the emotions as they flicker across his face. My heart feels full as I reach out and smooth a lock of hair off his forehead.

My heart doesn't seem to ache anymore; instead, I feel a wave of hope. It's a foolish hope, and I know it. But I can't seem to shake the joy bubbling inside of me. A feeling that everything is going to be all right.

Thirty-Six

Michael

It's Monday and I'm getting antsy waiting for Frank Zappo to contact me. I've heard from Trent's FBI contact; we have everything lined up. Now, we just need Frank.

My cell phone rings. I glance at the unknown number, and I immediately answer.

"Michael Garret," I answer.

Silence greets me. I wait. Impatience gnawing at me, but I don't give in to it.

"Michael, it's me." I sag against my desk as I hear Frank Zappo's voice.

THIRTY-SIX

"Frank. I'm glad you're alive," I say with relief.

"Yeah, but for how long?" he mutters gruffly.

"Frank, the FBI—" I begin.

"No! Not the FBI. Just you," he interrupts earnestly.

"But Frank, the FBI, they can protect you."

"Oh yeah? Then why didn't they?" he fires back.

"Alright. Listen—just you and me. You pick the place, and I'll be there," I tell him.

"Okay. The seafood restaurant where we met once. But behind it, in the alley. Ten o'clock tonight. Come alone."

Then I hear a click and stare down at my phone. Frank disconnected the call.

I reach for my desk phone to call Trent's contact with the FBI, but I keep hearing the desperation in Frank's voice. The suspicious way he questioned why they didn't protect him. I pull back my hand.

He said to come alone.

It's dark in the alley behind the seafood restaurant. I peer again at my watch. Frank said ten o'clock, and it's now eleven minutes later. I'll give him another five minutes.

I squint against the darkness. Did that shadow just move? A chill runs down my spine. It moves again and comes closer, morphing into the silhouette of a man. I finally see Frank Zappo's dim outline. He's dressed all in black, and for a minute, I'm not sure if he's an illusion or real.

"Michael. Are you alone?" he asks in a low, urgent voice.

I nod, and realizing he can't make out anything in the inky darkness, I say firmly, "Yes. I'm alone."

"Connie told me what you said. Who else knows I'm alive?"

"Only me, my team, Trent Goldman, and Joe Collins with the FBI."

"Joe Collins? I... I think he's clean. Hell, I don't even know anymore. Who's Trent Goldman?"

"He can be trusted. Joe approached him with information," I state in a low voice.

I glance around uneasily as something rustles in the bushes. A rat scurries past us, and I let out the breath I was holding.

"Frank, who were you going to testify against? This is important; I need to know."

"Someone in the Mexican cartel. I did a job for the Mazaranos down in Miami and saw something I shouldn't have. I wasn't even involved in what went down. But I was there in the warehouse and saw..." his voice trails off. "Anyway, when both deals went south, it was a cluster fuck. I was arrested."

Frank's narrative comes to an abrupt halt.

He takes a deep breath before he continues, "The FBI leaned on me. Hard. They're trying to get to the Mexican cartel. Put them away."

We're both quiet, as what he told me sinks in.

"And the body in the morgue?" I press him.

He gives a short laugh.

"Some poor bastard that happened to be in the wrong place at the wrong time. I was supposed to meet someone from the Mazaranos mob at the loading docks. Instead, the cartel got wind that I would be there and tried to take me out." I hear him sigh. "Instead, they killed some vagrant. It looked like he was homeless."

"And Victor Mazarano?"

"Michael, I have no fucking clue why Victor was there. He and Vito never show their faces. They let their lackeys do the heavy lifting."

"What happened next?" I ask, trying to see his expression through the dim gloom.

"All hell broke loose. Once shots rang out, the guy with the cartel confirmed the hit and then took off, and so did Victor. I laid low until they left. Then I checked out the body. That's when I got the idea to make people believe it was me. That way, the cartel thinks I'm dead, and I'd be free of the Mazaranos."

Frank leans in closer. "Michael, I don't know how the cartel knew I would be there that night. Unless someone in the FBI is dirty and set me up." I can hear the scorn in his voice.

I state grimly, "Victor was picked up because a camera caught his car driving away. He was meeting someone at the docks that night himself. When I asked who, he refused to tell me. He said it wasn't relevant to the case."

"Michael. I'm scared. I thought this would be my way out from under the Mazaranos. But now? I'm screwed."

"Frank, let me do some more digging. I'd like to speak to Joe Collins and tell him what happened. Do you think we can trust him?"

THIRTY-SIX

"Yes, I think so. I don't believe Joe was involved because I didn't tell him I would be at the docks that night. I told another guy named Harvey in his unit. If anyone's dirty, it's probably him," he says in disgust.

We discuss how we'll contact each other going forward, and with a quick handshake, we each slip away into the night.

When I arrive home later, the house is dark. I head wearily upstairs. I silently undress and crawl into bed without turning on the light. I'm quiet, being careful not to wake a sleeping Honey.

But as I shut my eyes, she whispers, "Did everything go alright tonight?"

"Yeah. Sorry, I didn't mean to wake you."

She states softly, "I couldn't sleep. I was worried about you." She rolls closer.

"I'm here now. Go back to sleep, sweetheart."

I wrap my arms around her. I hear a small sigh slip from her lips, and then she rests her head against my chest. I feel her lips brush gently across my skin. I smile and return the kiss softly on her forehead.

Within moments, the sound of Honey's deep, steady breathing lets me know that she's sleeping soundly. Holding her safely in my arms, I wonder how everything will come together. It has to work out. I feel the same urgent need as Frank to get away from the Mazarano crime family.

My mind continues to churn with all the what-ifs and how-comes. What was Victor doing at the docks that night? Who was he meeting? Is he hiding something? As the thoughts race through my mind, a sense of steely determination sweeps over me. I will solve this case. I will exonerate Victor, and finally, my family and I will be free of the Mazarano's reach.

Trent sets up a meeting with Joe Collins, the FBI agent we hope we can trust. A stubborn Trent insists on going with me, even though I don't want him involved.

We meet at a downtown diner. When Trent and I arrive, we warily glance around the place. It's mostly empty, except for a few lone patrons hunched over their meals. Joe is sitting in the last booth, his back to the wall.

We slip across from him into the booth. Instead of shaking hands, we exchange grim nods as Trent makes the introductions.

"Joe Collins, Michael Garret."

THIRTY-SIX

The waitress comes over, looking as if she's spent years in this place, her youth drained away. She barely acknowledges us as we order coffee and water, then shuffles off.

A few moments later, the waitress sets down our drinks and walks away with an indifferent smile. Joe leans forward after another quick sweep of the place to make sure no one is paying attention to our conversation.

"We're still interested in Frank testifying. The offer of protection stands," he states quietly.

"Frank doesn't trust an agent named Harvey," I say in a grim voice. "He was the only one who knew Frank would be at the docks that night. Frank thinks he was set up."

Joe's expression doesn't change.

"You don't seem surprised," I note, watching him closely.

"I'm not," he glowers, eyes darkening. "I've suspected Harvey for a while. This confirms he's in bed with the Mexican cartel." He drums his fingers on the table, clearly agitated.

After a moment, he leans in closer. "We can use this to our advantage. I could leak that Zappo is alive. Bait Harvey and the cartel."

"No. Absolutely not. I won't agree with using Frank as bait. There's no reason to," I point out. "Harvey and the cartel still believe Frank is dead. Correct?"

Joe frowns, considering. "Yes. I'm the only person in the agency who suspects Zappo made it."

I frown. "Nobody else knows?" I ask sharply.

"No." Joe shrugs. "We were talking off the record. Just two guys chatting. Neither of us was wired."

"Then you don't need to risk Frank," I say, my voice firm. "You could leak that you've got another witness from that warehouse in Miami."

Joe's fingers tap against the table again. Then his eyes light up. "Yeah. I could spin that. Draw them out."

"Good," I say, nodding. "Once Harvey's out of the way, Frank can resurface, and the charges against Victor Mazarano get dropped. But Harvey has to go down first."

Joe nods, then straightens in his seat. "I'll get the ball rolling," he assures us.

I lean in. "We need to move fast. I can't exonerate Victor until Frank can testify he wasn't involved in the murder at the docks."

THIRTY-SIX

Joe's eye ticks in a tell-tale sign. I lean forward. "You know why Victor was there, don't you?"

Joe glances around uneasily, his face unreadable.

I lower my voice. "I represent Victor. Attorney-client privilege."

Joe's eyes dart to Trent, who clears his throat. "I'll wait in the car," Trent says, standing and leaving without a word.

When the door swings shut, Joe leans closer and, in a low voice, says, "Victor isn't like his father. He wants out. That night, he was meeting me to turn over valuable information. Unfortunately, I had a flat and got there too late."

Understanding dawns as the pieces click into place. "So, you know Victor is innocent."

Joe nods grimly. "But his father can never know. If Vito finds out Victor's working with us, it's over for him."

Thirty-Seven

Michael

The next few days are torture. All I can do is wait. Time drags, each minute stretching out painfully, the silence pressing in like a weight on my chest. Every ring of the phone and every email notification makes my pulse spike, only to be followed by crushing disappointment when it's not the news I need.

I find myself pacing the office, my thoughts tangled in a web of possibilities and worst-case scenarios. The usual distractions—case files, meetings, even small talk—do nothing to ease the tension. It's as if the entire world has slowed down, leaving me in this unbearable limbo.

THIRTY-SEVEN

Waiting for a break. Waiting for a call. Waiting for the truth to finally come to light.

I notice the unease creeping into our home. Honey knows me better than anyone, and I can tell she senses something big is about to happen. Even the kids seem to pick up on the tension in the air, giving me more quiet glances than usual.

Tonight, after the kids are in bed, Honey and I sit together on the couch, the TV on, but neither of us is paying attention. She snuggles into my side, resting her head on my chest. Her warmth, her presence, it's the only thing that keeps me grounded. I feel her fingers tracing absent patterns on my arm, and I know she's waiting for me to open up.

"You've been distant," she says softly, without accusation, just concern. "Talk to me, Michael. I know something's weighing on you. I know it's about the case."

I wrap my arm around her tighter, inhaling the familiar scent of her floral perfume.

"I just... have a lot on my mind." I lean down to kiss her forehead, needing the comfort as much as I want to give it. "But you don't need to worry. Once this is over, I'll have all the time in the world for you, the baby, and the kids. I promise."

She lifts her head to look at me, her eyes searching mine, trying to decipher the truth beneath the vague reassurances. I lean in and kiss her softly, hoping to convey what words can't. Her lips move against mine slowly, lovingly, like she's trying to tell me it'll all be okay.

The world outside fades for a moment, and it's just us. But even as we pull apart, her hand rests on my cheek, and I know she's not convinced.

"We're in this together, Michael. Remember that," she whispers.

She takes my hand and pulls me upstairs. That night, Honey makes love to me. The lovemaking is slow and almost soothing—with no sense of urgency. It's her way of keeping my mind off of my troubles. She's always so giving of her love, and yet I... I don't give her any love in return. The thought filters through my mind, causing me to question everything. But I don't have time to dwell on it. Not until this mess is over. Maybe then, I can examine the promise I made to myself. Maybe then, I'll have more to offer, Honey. But for now, my entire being is focused on one thing. Waiting.

The next night, it's late, and the office is finally still. After hours of pacing and staring at the same document, I give in to the exhaustion and sit, elbows propped on my desk in the dim light. My phone sits beside me, motionless. Always silent. I try to convince myself to head home.

Then, the phone vibrates.

My heart jumps into my throat as I see Joe's name flash across the screen. For a split second, I hesitate. My hand hovers over the phone, knowing that whatever news he's about to give me could change everything.

I swipe the screen. "Joe?"

His voice is sharp. "We got him."

My grip tightens on the phone. "Harvey?"

"Yes, Harvey. It's done. He's in custody. Frank's safe." There's a moment of silence. "But you need to move fast. This news won't stay quiet for long."

I hang up the phone, feeling the weight of it all lift from my shoulder, hardly daring to believe that it might finally be over. I rest my head against my chair, but only for a moment. I abruptly straighten and, taking a deep breath, I eagerly pick up the phone. It's about time for me to inform everyone of the good news.

In a dramatic turn of events, my case becomes major headline news. The shocking revelations dominate the network stations, marking this as one of the most explosive developments in recent legal history.

News anchors quickly recap the saga, highlighting Frank Zappo's unexpected reappearance and debunking previous reports of his death. The media buzzes with speculation about the implications for the Mazarano crime family and the Mexican cartel, with some questioning how deep FBI corruption might go.

"Inside sources suggest a high-ranking FBI agent may have been involved in a cover-up," one anchor reported, as grainy footage of Harvey being led away in handcuffs played across the screen.

While the media frenzy continued, I was able to get Victor Mazarano's case officially dismissed. The verdict felt almost anti-climactic. It seemed too easy, as you can't be accused of murder if the victim is alive.

I can finally leave the tension behind. For the first time in weeks, I start to breathe easily, thinking all of this is behind us.

THIRTY-SEVEN

But my lingering sense of unease doesn't escape me. Even as everything settles back to normal, I still feel like something is hanging over my head, unresolved. I can't shake the feeling and find myself glancing over my shoulder more than once. Even the children sense it.

Last night, I heard Megan pull Honey aside and whisper, "Is Dad, okay? He looks...worried."

Honey assured her everything was fine, but my mind knew better. Something still feels ... off.

The next afternoon, it happens. I leave the office to meet Trent for a late lunch when a sleek, black car pulls up beside me. A man I don't recognize steps out, dressed in an immaculate suit, his expression unreadable. At first, there's no sense of danger—just formality—but my instincts tell me something is terribly wrong.

"Michael Garret?" he asks as if confirming my identity is just a formality. He gestures to the car behind him, the door already open. "Mr. Vito Mazarano would like to speak with you. It's important."

My heart skips a beat. I hesitate. Maybe he just wants to thank me. I try to convince myself.

The gentleman steps closer, his voice polite but firm. "There's no reason to be alarmed, Mr. Garret. But Mr. Mazarano insists."

A sense of danger grips me, but I nod, keeping my voice steady as I respond. "Alright."

He nods, standing quietly by the door. As I slide onto the seat, I feel the smoothness of the high-quality leather, but the arrogant look in Vito Mazarano's eyes warns me I won't like what he has to say.

Vito nods, "Mr. Garret. I am extremely pleased with the outcome of my son's case."

I give a relieved nod. Maybe he does just want to thank me.

"In fact. I would like you to consider representing me and my interests exclusively."

His words echo in the small interior, shattering any belief that my connection to the Mazarano crime family is over.

"Mr. Mazarano, while I appreciate the offer. I have to decline," I say, carefully choosing my words.

He gives me a superior smile. "I thought that might be your answer. Maybe you would like a chance to talk it over with your wife?"

THIRTY-SEVEN

As I start to shake my head, he ignores me and says in a low voice. "Charles, can you get Mrs. Garret on the phone, please?"

I watch as the driver punches in numbers, and Honey's voice fills the car.

"Hello?" she answers, her voice shaking.

I frown. "Honey? Where are you?"

"Michael! I'm at the Mazarano estate. They sent a car for me. Vito Mazarano requested I eat lunch with him."

My eyes fly to Vito, and he smiles slyly. I suddenly find it hard to breathe as a weight settles heavily in my chest. "Honey, I'm sure everything is fine. Just," I stop to clear my throat, "Just do whatever they tell you. Okay? I'm going to talk to Vito Mazarano now."

"Alright, Michael." The line goes dead.

"You may leave now, Mr. Garret. I've already had the papers drawn up. I expect you to be at my house tomorrow for dinner at six o'clock. In the meantime, your wife will be my houseguest."

He stops to arrogantly adjust his tie. "We'll take very good care of her. I know she's expecting, so we wouldn't want to do anything that might jeopardize her health or the baby's."

Vito gives me a direct look. "Would we?"

I grimly shake my head. I push open the car door and step out.

Vito rolls down the window. "One more thing, Mr. Garret. Your wife is worried about not being able to pick up your children. I assured her you'd handle their safety."

With those parting words, they drive away.

I'm stunned. Almost numb. I'll get the children. But my mind is on Honey. She's alone and being held by the leader of the mob. My heart aches for her... she has to be terrified. I wish I could have said more. I know this isn't a kidnapping, but the cold, calculated way this is happening leaves me with no doubt: Vito Mazarano isn't playing games. Honey is in danger.

I feel my heart begin to pound as I realize I could lose Honey and the child she's carrying. I try to block out the panic and agony of my thoughts as I hurriedly walk half a block to the restaurant where Trent is waiting. The minute I sit down, he frowns.

"Michael, what's wrong?" he demands.

"Vito Mazarano wants me to work exclusively for him as his attorney."

"Can you just tell him no—"

THIRTY-SEVEN

I cut Trent off. "He has Honey," I blurt out. "I was escorted to his car, and he called her. She's okay for now." A shutter courses through me. "He said she'll be his guest. I have until six o'clock tomorrow."

Trent stands. "Come on."

I glance at him in surprise but stand and follow him out of the restaurant.

"Where are we going?" I ask as we head to his car.

"My grandmothers," he states without explaining anything more.

When we arrive at Skipper's, Trent rings the bell.

Once Skipper answers the door, she takes one look at our sober faces and hurries us in.

"What's happened?" She asks.

Trent quickly begins to fill her in as we follow her into her kitchen. She quietly gets us a glass of sweet iced tea and listens intently without interrupting.

As Trent finishes, he looks at her expectantly. "Well, Grandmother?"

"I'm glad you came to me. Let me make a phone call."

Skipper gets out her phone and dials. I sit there, my mind reeling. Who is she calling, and how will they be able to help?

"Hi, Ezra. I need to speak to Brian or Lock."

I start to shake my head. "No, Skipper, don't get them involved—"

Trent grabs my arm, and Skipper smiles to reassure me.

Skipper then puts the phone on speaker, and we hear Lock answer.

"Skipper. What can I do for you?"

"I was hoping Brixx and Lochlain might be able to help. Put me on speaker, please."

I raise my eyebrow at Trent, but he just grins. We hear a few muffled sounds, and Lock states, "Go ahead, Skipper."

"Vito Mazarano has Honey. He's trying to pressure Michael into signing a contract that will bind them to the Mazarano family."

"I see." The harsh voice almost sounds like Honey's grandfather. That's all the words he utters, but the voice is hard. Brutal. It sends a chill up my spine.

THIRTY-SEVEN

"How much time do we have?" Lock asks quietly, his tone stony.

"Six o'clock tomorrow evening," Skipper states.

"I'll handle Vito. We'll be at your house by four."

"Thank you," Skipper says in a relieved voice.

"No, thank you. I won't allow him to mess with my family."

Thirty-Eight

EARLIER THAT DAY

Honey

I don't have a choice.

I feel a knot tighten in my stomach as I follow the unknown man into the car, my heart pounding faster with every mile that passes. I'm not scared—at least, not for myself—but I know Vito Mazarano doesn't make casual invitations. This is about Michael. It has to be.

When we arrive at the sprawling estate, I'm escorted into a grand dining room. Vito is waiting, sitting at the head of the

THIRTY-EIGHT

table with a glass of wine in his hand. His smile is warm, but his eyes stay sharp and calculating.

"Mrs. Garret... or may I call you Honey?" he greets smoothly, gesturing for me to sit across from him. "Thank you for accepting my invitation."

I force a smile and a nod as I sink into the chair, my thoughts spinning, every fiber of my being on edge. What does he want?

"It's simple," Vito continues, his voice smooth as silk. "I'm quite pleased with Michael's work on my son's case. In fact, I'd like him to represent me exclusively moving forward."

His words land like a sledgehammer, and it takes all my strength to keep my expression neutral. I blink, struggling to gain my composure. "I don't think that's something Michael would agree to," I manage, my voice steady, but inside, I'm reeling.

Vito's smile doesn't waver, but it never reaches his eyes. "I expected as much, which is why you're here, Honey. I think you understand how much your husband values you. He wouldn't want anything to happen to you or your family."

The unspoken threat hangs in the air, choking any semblance of calm I have left. I force myself to meet his gaze, refusing to show fear.

"Michael won't be bullied," I say, keeping my voice soft but firm.

His smile deepens as he leans back, clearly enjoying the power play.

"We'll see. For now, you'll be my guest. I'm sure Michael will reconsider once he knows you're here."

"The children. I have to pick them up from school—"

Vito interrupts me smoothly. "I'm leaving to speak with your husband now," he says. "He'll have plenty of time to make arrangements for their safety."

And with that, he leaves me alone in the cavernous room, the echo of his footsteps fading.

The night drags on, filled with tension. Tossing and turning, I finally surrender to exhaustion and slip into a restless sleep. Vito had a silk nightgown and robe delivered to my room. I didn't want to touch it. But after laying down in my clothes, I had second thoughts and put it on. The luxurious fabric feels soft against my skin, but it only reminds me of where I'm at as it clings to my skin.

THIRTY-EIGHT

In the morning, a shiver runs down my spine when I discover my clothes are gone. Someone entered my room while I was sleeping.

When the knock comes, I almost jump. A maid enters with my freshly laundered clothes and hands them over with a polite, indifferent smile.

The day stretches endlessly as I wander the manicured gardens, never far from the eyes of a discreet security guard. The tension is getting to me, the sense of danger ever-present, but there's nothing to do but wait.

I glance again at the clock. It's almost six—Michael's deadline.

Vito Mazarano walks in, followed by his son, Victor.

"Mrs. Garret," Victor greets me, his voice softer than I expect. "I apologize for this inconvenience."

Victor doesn't say anything more, but there's something in his eyes. I get a sense of regret. I could almost believe he's sorry that I'm here.

A butler-turned-security guard interrupts, announcing Michael's arrival.

The moment he enters, my heart leaps. "Michael," I stammer, relief flooding through me as he rushes toward me, pulling me into his strong arms.

"Honey. Thank God you're alright," he murmurs, holding me tightly.

But as I look around, confusion creeps in. Trent is with him—along with my grandfather and Lock. The air shifts as they approach, the tension in the room spiking.

"Grandpa?" I turn toward him, baffled.

My grandfather's eyes sharply rake me from head to toe. Only once he's ensured that I'm okay does he give me a fond smile. Lock stands tall beside him, silent but imposing.

Vito glances from my grandfather to Lock, and then his eyes widen.

"Lochlain, is that you?" I hear the disbelief in his voice. His eyes dart back to my grandfather, and his expression falters. "Brixx? I almost didn't recognize you... Your hair, it's white." I hear the stunned shock in his voice.

My grandfather nods, his presence suddenly larger than life. "It's been a long time, Vito," he says quietly, his voice cutting through the room.

THIRTY-EIGHT

"Yes, it has... it's been years. Everyone thought you were dead. You just disappeared." Vito murmurs in a low voice.

"As you can see, I'm very much alive," my grandfather says with a scoff. Then his gaze hardens, and in a steely voice, "You have my granddaughter."

Vito looks taken aback. "Honey, is your granddaughter?" His eyes dart to me and then back to my grandfather. "I didn't know, Brixx." He looks uncomfortable.

Without breaking eye contact my grandfather reaches into his pocket and pulls out a small blue poker chip. He holds it up for Vito to see. His voice drops to a dangerous murmur.

"Vito, I have a blood oath marker here. Your guarantee that no member of my family would ever be touched as long as you live."

Vito Mazarano's face goes pale. He swallows heavily as his eyes flicker from the chip to my grandfather. "I... yes. I honor my blood oath, Brixx. I didn't know Honey was related to you."

"Not just Honey, she's a Garret now. That means the Garrets are my family, also."

My grandfather cocks an eyebrow at Vito, his gaze steady and unyielding. Vito shifts from one foot to the other, clearly uncomfortable. Michael and I exchange wide-eyed glances, the unspoken realization between us—Vito, the man who commands so much power, is intimidated by my grandfather.

"Understood," Vito says, his voice steady, but there's a flicker of hesitation in his eyes. He rubs his hands together and asks in a smoother voice, "You'll be staying for dinner?"

Grandpa turns to me, raising a brow. "Mary Catherine? Would you prefer we leave or stay?"

A warm smile spreads across my face as I meet his gaze. "I think we should stay, Grandpa. I'm sure you and Vito would enjoy the chance to talk about old times."

A twinkle lights up my grandfather's eyes, and he nods. "Humph. Alright then. Yes, Vito, we'll be staying for dinner."

"Excellent." Vito nods and turns, leading the way into the elegant dining room.

Michael reaches over and gently takes my hand in his. His gaze, almost loving, warms me.

We sit mostly in silence as dinner progresses, listening carefully. The more my grandfather and Lock speak, the more pieces fall into place. My grandfather is Irish—something I always knew—but now I see him in a completely different light. His

THIRTY-EIGHT

hair, now snow white, used to be red. Occasionally, a faint Irish lilt creeps into his voice, a reminder of his origins.

I knew he grew up in Philadelphia. He'd tell us stories, funny anecdotes about Philly, the rough streets, and the "gang" he ran with. But I never knew—never even guessed—that he was once the leader of the Philly Irish mob. The rumors I'd heard over the years about my family's mob ties had always seemed just that—rumors.

But now, sitting here, it's undeniable. My sweet, slightly frail Grandpa is a man feared by people like Vito Mazarano. The realization shocks me to my core, and questions start flooding my mind. These are questions I'm not sure I want answered. What did he do? What kind of life did he lead? What terrible things has he seen—or done?

But I push the thoughts away, forcing myself to focus on the present. It's easier, and safer not to dig too deep into the darkness of the past. Some things, I realize, are better left buried.

Thirty-Nine

Michael

My arm immediately wraps around Honey, and I pull her close to me in the car. Needing to feel her warmth pressed against me, needing to know she's safe. I do not want to let her out of my sight.

It's late by the time we reach Skipper's house. She and Paige meet us at the door. Their faces lighting up with relief as they swing the door wide.

"Glad you're all back safely," Skipper murmurs with a proud glance at my grandfather.

She grimaces slightly. "Sorry, the cats out of the bag."

THIRTY-NINE

My grandfather gives her a brief hug. "Skipper, I'm glad you called."

Lock, standing a bit behind, gives my grandfather a solemn look before saying, "Let's get you to bed, sir."

My Grandpa grins, his energy still sparking. "It was like old times, wasn't it, Lock?"

Lock's face breaks into a rare smile. "Yes, it was."

I watch as Lock gently leads him up the stairs, their shared history unspoken but obvious.

Skipper turns to Honey and me, her voice soft. "The children are sleeping. Why don't you leave them here for the night?"

Honey and I both nod. "Thanks, Aunt Skip." Honey leans in and gives her aunt a heartfelt hug.

"You'll let me know if you have any more skeletons in the closet, won't you?" Honey teases, her voice carrying just loud enough for everyone to hear.

Skipper just gives a tinkling laugh as Paige and Trent frown at his grandmother's non-committal answer.

On the ride home, silence settles between Honey and me, thick with everything left unsaid. Both of us are too shaken to voice what we're truly thinking—what could've happened if her grandfather hadn't had that blood oath marker.

As we head directly up the steps and into our bedroom, I still think about what Vito could have done to Honey. My eyes watch her tenderly as she undresses and then slowly crawls into bed. I slide in beside her and gently pull her into my arms. The warmth of her is a reassurance I've needed all night.

"Michael, I'm alright. Nothing happened," she whispers, her voice soft yet steady.

A sigh escapes my lips. "I know."

I tighten my hold around her, words tumbling out before I can stop them.

"Honey... I've tried so hard to guard my heart from you. After Michelle, I swore I'd never let myself feel that kind of loss again. I didn't think I could survive it if I opened myself up to that type of pain a second time."

Honey gently pulls away and looks up at me with her big brown eyes, which seem to shimmer with fragile hope.

"Honey," I begin, my voice steady this time, "what I'm trying to say is that I love you."

THIRTY-NINE

As her eyes suddenly fill with tears, I reach down and kiss her softly, lovingly.

"I was worried I wouldn't get the chance to tell you," I admit, my voice thick with emotion.

"I've cared for you for quite a while, almost as soon as you started working for me. You walked into my family and filled our home with your bright smile. It was like a beam of sunshine that helped chase the gloom away, the sorrow. At the time, I was still too filled with grief over Michelle."

Honey's eyes turn sad, and she nods, understanding without needing more words.

"But you helped us heal," I say, my voice soft. "I started looking forward to our late-night talks after the kids went to bed. I slowly started to notice you. So slowly that I didn't realize it at first. It was little things like how you cared for us, how you cooked a meal, how you made us feel like a family again. Then I started noticing you as a woman."

I grimace at the memory. "That summer when we went tubing, I didn't have very employer-like thoughts when I saw you in that one-piece swimsuit. I told myself you were off-limits. But the truth? I didn't want to lose you. I kept convincing myself I was holding back for the kids... but I was really scared of how much I needed you. Wanted you."

Honey listens quietly, her eyes never leaving mine as I pour out everything I've kept locked inside for so long.

"I knew I cared about you, but I foolishly thought I could ignore the need I had for you. The night Matthew broke his arm. I was so jealous. I lost my temper, and then I lost control...because I couldn't keep pretending anymore. I gave in to my cravings—I couldn't deny what I felt anymore."

"I tried my best to deny my feelings. I told you it was a mistake, and I meant it at the time. But when I found out you were pregnant. It was a shock, yes, but it was also a relief. It gave me a reason to marry you—a reason to keep you close. I was selfish enough to take everything you gave me – without giving you very much back."

Honey is silent, but I know she's listening to the words that pour out of me like a dam bursting.

"When Vito threatened you. I realized that no matter how hard I'd tried to guard my heart... you managed to slip past all of my defenses so deeply that I don't feel whole without you anymore. I need you, Honey. I love you very much."

THIRTY-NINE

My words hang in the air, heavy with the truth I've kept buried for too long.

"My love for you is different from how I loved Michelle, but that doesn't mean it isn't as deep—as powerful. The love I feel for you is the forever kind. I never thought I'd feel that way again... but I do."

I look down at her, watching as silent tears slide down her cheeks, and she gives me a watery smile.

"Honey, please forgive me for not telling you this sooner."

I cup her face with my hands, then rain kisses across her tear-streaked face, over her wet lashes, her cheeks, her forehead, her chin, every inch of her beautiful face.

Then I slowly take her lips with mine. I savor her sweet, honey-like taste. When I raise my head, her eyes are shining with love, mirroring everything I feel in my own eyes.

"Oh, Michael," she whispers, her voice thick with emotion. "I've longed for you to say those words, to return my love. My heart feels so full."

"I know, sweetheart," I whisper, gently brushing her hair back. "I feel the same."

I kiss her again, only deeper, as my passion starts to rise.

"I want to make love to you, Honey. Love. But I think you already knew that every time we came together, it was making love."

She smiles up at me, "I hoped it was, Michael."

I roll her underneath me. "I love you so much, Honey. Now, let me show you how much."

As I reach for her with reverence, I know that we have all night and all of our tomorrows, as well. This moment, and this love we've fought so hard to protect, is ours forever.

Epilogue

Michael

I glance down at Honey in the hospital bed, our baby girl nestled tenderly in her arms. I gently brush Honey's sweat-soaked hair back from her face.

"How are you feeling?" I ask her softly.

She gives me a tired smile. "Worn out but wonderful."

Honey looks lovingly down at our small daughter. "She's perfect. Isn't she, Michael?"

"Perfect," I agree. "Just like her mother."

Honey glances at me, her eyes shining. "Can Megan and Matthew come in to see her?"

"Yes, but I told them they couldn't touch or hold her yet."

I walk over to the door, open it, and wave the children in.

They look wide-eyed at the newborn in Honey's arms. They both look at her with wonder shimmering in their eyes.

Honey smiles as she positions the baby so they can see her face.

"Megan and Matthew, meet your baby sister, Mary Michelle Garret."

Later, when we bring the baby home. Honey and I stand at the crib, watching our little girl sleep. The soft yellow of the walls and bright white furniture give the room a cozy feel. The wooly little lamb, our baby's first gift, sits in a place of honor atop the dresser.

I reach out and turn on the baby monitor, yet neither of us is in any hurry to leave the room.

"She's so precious," Honey whispers.

"Yes, she is," I murmur softly.

I turn and pull Honey into my arms.

"I love you, Honey. Thank you for showing me how to love again. And for giving me another child to love."

Honey melts against me with a sigh, and my heart fills to overflowing with the love I feel for her. We hear a muffled sound behind us, and I turn to see Megan and Matthew peeking in.

I wave them over, and we share a warm group hug, our eyes on the sweetly sleeping baby in the crib.

Matthew says, "Our family just keeps getting bigger and bigger."

Then he turns to me. "Dad, can you and Honey have a boy next time?" His eyes hopeful.

I chuckle as I look at Honey, my eyes filled with love. "Matthew, I can't make any promises, but we'll certainly try."

The End.

Did you like this Book?

Then you'll love FALLING TOO HARD

[Want to continue reading this series? Go to the first book in Illegal Affairs II: Fake Fiancée for the Billionaire]

FALLING TOO HARD

The first full-sized book in the TOO SERIES

(Maggie and Jaxson's Story)

Jaxson is a grumpy, hot-tempered, sexy P.I. used to nabbing the bad guys.

That is no excuse for him to accuse me of stealing his luggage!

After he almost got me arrested at the airport, I truly hate the man!

Sexy, arrogant men are so not worth my time!

I'm a fiery redhead with a temper to match. We're like oil and water.

I've sworn off men and made a promise to myself and all my friends - No more relationships!

Jaxson and I can't stand each other but we can't seem to keep our hands off each other either.

So, he agrees to my terms: A 'good time only, no strings attached' torrid affair.

But the more I'm around him, the more my heart is in danger of getting broken.

By a man that I hate, or do I?

Start reading Falling Too Hard NOW!

Sneak Peek - Chapter One

Jaxson

I get to the conveyor belt at the Jacksonville International Airport a little late, as there was an older couple in front of me, and the woman had a walker, so I didn't want to rush them.

That saying 'no good deed goes unpunished' stays with me as I now have to hurry to find my luggage. I'm tired and grumpy after my flight was delayed. I just want to get home and take a long hot shower and have a beer.

I really enjoy my job as a private investigator most of the time, but this last case reminds me of just how untrustworthy people can be. It's left me feeling cynical and suspicious of everyone's motives.

I look around and can't find my suitcase. I'm pissed because I typically only travel with a carry-on, but again I was being a nice guy when the ticketing girl, who appeared painfully new, made a mistake. I just went with it. Damn it. Where the hell is my suitcase? There are no more pieces of luggage coming down the belt. My suitcase is a dark blue paisley design that is unique enough that I can usually spot it pretty easily.

My eyes dart around the area, and I notice a pair of mile-long legs attached to a perfect ass. My eyes continue up to an hour-glass figure in ass-hugging jeans and a blouse. I can't see her face, but she has pulled her long red hair back in a ponytail that sways as she's hurrying towards the doors. That's when I finally notice my suitcase is being wheeled away by the little tart.

"Hey, you, Red," I say in a semi-shout. I see her steps falter, and then she turns hesitantly around.

"That's my suitcase you're trying to lift." I accuse her.

"Lift?" She tries to act confused.

"Lift, pilfer, snatch, grab." At her still-confused look, I make it clear. "Steal."

"Steal?" She looks incredulously at me. "Are you implying that I'm trying to steal my own suitcase?"

"Yes, don't play dumb with me." I reach for the handle, which should have the white plastic airline tag they put around it, and it's not there.

"This is my suitcase," she says firmly, then looks down at the wheels and says with uncertainty and a little apologetically.

"Oh, the wheels do look slightly different..."

"Yeah, I just bet they do," I say dryly and accusingly.

She turns and glares up at me. Her eyes are a deep emerald green, and right now, they are hot enough to start a fire.

"Why are you acting like a jerk? If this is your suitcase and not mine, then obviously I've made an honest mistake. I'm sure we can work this out." She moves a little closer to the conveyor belt that is no longer in motion.

"Yeah, right? Why don't I just call over a security guard now, or better yet, the cops?" I state firmly, to see how she'll react to that. If she's done this before, that should make her nervous. I grab the handle of the suitcase and pull it in front of me.

She doesn't bat an eye; I watch as a furious red colors her cheeks with her anger, and she doesn't resist me taking my suitcase. Instead, she straightens her back, which pushes out her chest so that I notice her generous breasts. Another move by an expert, I think grimly.

Right then, the conveyor belt starts to move, and one lone blue paisley piece of wheeled luggage comes out on the belt. We both watch it as it slowly makes its way over to where we are now standing.

She places her hand on her hip and puts the full force of her anger in a glance as she lifts an eyebrow with an 'I told you so' superior look as she lifts her chin.

She then reaches out as the luggage comes around and pulls it off the belt.

I watch as she reaches down to the white airline tag and turns it over. Satisfied it is hers, she stands and turns to me with a self-righteous air and states: "There was absolutely no reason for you to act like such an ass. But that's what I'd expect from a Neanderthal like you," Her eyes look me up and down disapprovingly. "All brawn and no brains," she states with a superior sneer, and with that parting shot, she dismisses me. She self-righteously turns and marches out of the terminal without once glancing back.

Start reading Falling Too Hard NOW!

Do you like FREEBIE Romance books?

Want to know who started the Too Series?

Sign up for my newsletter and get IN TOO DEEP for FREE!

(Haley and Jake's Story)

H.O.T. Playboy Billionaire Needs Fake Fiancée!

She's off-limits, but I'm about to make her mine.

What could possibly go wrong?

The Company Board of Directors makes it clear: Clean up my act!

So, when I'm caught in a compromising position, I do the only thing I can think of, I lie and tell the world we're engaged.

But here's the kicker.

Haley isn't just any woman. She's my best friend's younger sister and completely off-limits.

Now, we're playing house, pretending to be madly in love.

Yet, the more I try to keep my distance, the more I find myself drawn to her infectious laughter and fiery spirit.

And the biggest problem?

I might just be falling for her, and if my lies unravel, I could lose everything, including the only woman who's ever made me want to be more than just a playboy.

Sign Up Now! for my Free Book and Newsletter or Scan the QR Code Below:

In Too Deep & Newsletter Sign Up

Want to see the rest of my books? Click HERE! to see all of my books or Scan the QR Code Below:

Kelly Thomas All Books

Sign up for my Newsletter to be notified when my next book in this series goes live: Sign Up NOW!or Scan the QR Code Below:

DID YOU LIKE THIS BOOK?

Kelly
Thomas
Newsletter
Sign Up

Printed in Great Britain
by Amazon